THE STARS AT NOON

DENIS JOHNSON

THE

STARS

AT

NOON

 Alfred A. Knopf   New York   1986

THIS IS A BORZOI BOOK
PUBLISHED BY ALFRED A. KNOPF, INC.

Grateful acknowledgment is made to the following for permission to reprint
previously published material:

ATHENEUM PUBLISHERS, INC.: Excerpts from the poems "The Present,"
"Route With No Number," "To My Brother Hanson," "The Nails," and
"Bread and Butter" from *The Moving Target* by W. S. Merwin. Copyright
© 1960, 1961, 1962, 1963 by W. S. Merwin. Reprinted with the permission
of Atheneum Publishers, Inc.

GRAYWOLF PRESS: Excerpt from "Sunday Snow" from *The Salt Ecstasies*
by James L. White. © 1982 by James L. White. Reprinted by permission of
Graywolf Press.

Library of Congress Cataloging-in-Publication Data
Johnson, Denis, [date]
The stars at noon.
I. Title.
PS3560.0374S7   1986   813'.54   86-45274
ISBN 0-394-53840-4

Manufactured in the United States of America
First Edition

. . . what we are looking for
In each other
Is each other,

The stars at noon,

While the light worships its blind god.

W. S. MERWIN

ONE

THE AIR was getting thick—if you like calling a garotte of diesel and greasy dirt "air"—and so before the burning rain began I stepped into the McDonald's. But right away I caught sight of the grotesque troublemaker, the pitiful little fat person whose name was forever escaping me, Subtenente Whoever from Interpren, getting out of his black Czechoslovakian Skoda and standing there on the dark street with my fate in his hands . . . If I didn't go to bed with him again soon, he was going to lift my card.

I hoped it wasn't me he was waving at, but I was the only customer in the place. I've always been the only patron in the McDonald's here in this hated city, because with the meat shortage you wouldn't ever know absolutely, would you, what sort of a thing they were handing you in the guise of beef. But I don't care, actually, what I eat. I just want to lean on that characteristic McDonald's counter while they fail to take my order and read the eleven certifying documents on the wall above the broken ice-cream box, nine of them with the double-arch McDonald's symbol and the two most recent stamped with the encircled triangle and offering the pointless endorsement of the Junta Local de Asistancia Social de Nicaragua . . . It's the only Communist-run McDonald's ever. It's the only McDonald's where you have to give back your plastic cup so it can be washed out and used again, the only McDonald's staffed by people wearing military fatigues and carrying submachine guns.

I let go of my supper plans and headed for the ladies' room in the hallway leading to the kitchen.

The two soldiers leaning against the drinking fountain looked between me and the approaching Sub-tenente with slow eyes that said they understood what was happening and were completely bored by it.

I thought I'd wait him out in the ladies' room, doing nothing, only sweating—needless to say, I wouldn't go so far in such an environment as actually to raise my skirts and pee; and the walls were too damp to hold graffiti . . . I was sure the Sub-tenente hadn't got a good enough look to say it was me—

He came around anyway and stood outside the door and coughed.

"Señorita."

I turned on the faucet, but it didn't work.

"Señorita," Sub-tenente Whoever said.

I tried the toilet, which flushed but didn't refill . . . Just the same, the sight of a more or less genuine commode, with a handle and a cover-and-seat, functioning or not . . . Nothing fancy, but a lot of the lavatories down here don't have toilets, that is, the room itself is designed to be one monstrous toilet, with water running down the walls and gradually, over the course of days, influencing substances toward tiny plugged-up drains in the corners.

The Sub-tenente knocked on my door now. This seemed, all by itself, a slimy presumption. He cleared his throat . . . Costa Rica was just across the border. But they would never let me out of this country.

"Señorita," he said through the door, "may you tell to me if you are intending to remain very long?"

I looked for toilet paper, but there wasn't any toilet paper and there never would be toilet paper—south of here they were having a party with streamers of the stuff, miles and miles of toilet paper, but here in the hyper-new, all-leftist future coming at us at the rate of rock-n-roll there was just a lot of nothing, no more wiping your bum, no more Coca-Cola, no beans or rice: except for me they got no more shiny pants, no more spiked heels. No unslakeable thirst! No kissing while dancing! No whores! No meat! No milk! South of here was Paradise, average daily temperature 71° Fahrenheit, the light sad and harmless, virgins eating ice-cream cones walking up and down—

"Señorita, if possible I will wait for you . . ."

Still I thought I could hold out a few seconds longer, hugging the wall—drugged, like a little kid, by the taste of my own tears on my lips . . .

"Señorita. Señorita. Señorita," said the Sub-tenente.

He said something to the soldiers outside and everybody laughed.

"Sí. Sí. Sí," I said. I opened the door. "Sub-tenente Verga!" —which wasn't his name, but "verga" means *prick*—"It's so good to see you again!"

I DIDN'T think this would take long . . . And it didn't . . .

We were doing it on the couch tonight: it was either that or the rug . . . His clothes, civilian clothes, lay in a heap beside mine—I'd never seen Sub-tenente Whoever in uniform. He was a spy, or something like that. I believe anybody who thought about it would have said he affected the goat-like Lenin look, but in truth his features were unshaped, they seemed to be materializing out of a bright fog, nothing more than a shining blank with shadows floating on it . . . Even as he coasted back and forth above me with the lamp behind him, the oval of his face gave out a mysterious light, like the exit from a tunnel . . . "Are you looking at me," I asked him softly, but he was sighing and hiccuping too loudly to hear. I hoped he wouldn't go on long enough to make me sore. I started to worry that maybe I was too thin for him, it's a fact that I'm always either too fat or too skinny, I can't seem to locate the mid-point. Not that the pleasure and comfort of an incompetent small-time official in a floundering greasy banana regime surmounts my every concern, but all men tend to grow innocent, wouldn't you agree, at the breast . . . You can't help feeling a little something, if only a small sharp pity, as if you'd just stepped on a baby bird. The bird was going to die anyway, you only shortened its brainless misery . . . "Are you coming? Are you coming?" I was speaking English. He probably didn't know what I was talking about . . .

Through it all I wept and sniffled, I did it all the time, it was becoming a kind of trademark.

The Sub-tenente spoke softly, he stroked me, he was thankful, what a laugh, if only they knew how obvious they all are!

And here we languished perspiring in his bureaucratic tristoire with its slatted shutters, and also, even, a rug . . . Cozy . . . But in this climate generally you didn't want cozy. Anything but.

"Do you have any talcum powder?" I asked him.

Already he was engaging the routine—acting like he'd skipped some critical errand and couldn't remember what. "Qué?" Getting on his shirt like he was late for an appointment, and so on.

"Polvos de talco, baby?"

"Oh. Sí. Sí," and he started toward the bathroom, changed his mind. "No. No." He spoke in Spanish now: "Listen to me. I want to tell you something."

"Yes—"

"The moment has come when I must take your press card and your letter of authority."

"What are you saying?"

"You are not a journalist."

"But I am. Yes."

"No." He held my purse in one hand and searched through it with the other.

"Yes." I snatched the purse from him and he shuffled quickly through some papers his hand had come away clutching. He picked out the letter he'd written authorizing me to visit various locations in the capacity of a journalist.

I was naked, but I suppose that was my armor. He tossed my other papers on the bed and held out his hand, but didn't come at me.

"And your press card. It's necessary for me to ask for your press card also. *Also.*"

"I don't have it."

"Yes. You have it."

"It's in my room at the motel."

He shook his head. "No."

"You can't have it."

"Your press card is invalidated."

"Who invalidated it?"

"I am forced to do it."

"I don't understand." I was crying again as usual.

Hadn't we just made love? His brown eyes were small and hard. The guilt I saw in them was like a child's. It wasn't aware of itself.

"One of these days the army will arrest you," he said.

"Why are you doing this?"

"This letter carries my name. Everyone who reads it sees my name."

He swaggered a little, hefting the letter in his hand. As if taking it away had made him significant. Honestly, they're all pimps.

And so we stood out front, quite soon, as usual, waiting for my cab, my armpits feeling prickly and sweat that would never dry slipping down between my breasts. The wind shook the leaves around us on the dark street.

"I left many messages for you but you didn't responded. Why that is?" he said. "I am force, I am force to wonder."

While he tried for irony in his torn-phrasebook English, he was busy unlocking the gate in the iron fence to get his car out. The fence ran the length of the block before the row of flats.

Oh, their suspicions, the self-degrading fantasies, the panic in their hearts. Whatever his innuendos covered was bottomless. It went down from his mother's womb, I knew that by now. It had to do with the Devil, the Madonna, the Christ.

"I tried to call you," I said, "but the phones weren't working."

The office-cum-boudoir he had the use of was in a viny residential neighborhood I was already unfortunately acquainted with, even quite bored with; in fact all by itself the familiar groaning of its sap-fat branches readjusted by a breeze sickened me . . .

"I'll be needing some shampoo tomorrow at the Mercado," I said.

"I'll buy for you this shampoo. With much pleasure."

"You're very generous."

Now the Sub-tenente was embarrassed, and seemed to be suffering.

"You go ahead," I said. "I'm fine."

"If it is quite okay," he said, and hopped into his defunct Czech juntamobile and disappeared—all in as many seconds,

I swear to you, as it takes to say it—leaving behind that ragged small-car sound echoing in the carport.

He had nothing! nothing! nothing about him that was manly . . .

Oh, well. In his own way, he was nice to me.

Before too long an old Impala stopped for me, and the driver identified this vehicle as my cab. What a mutilated heap! In this place everything—the cars, the colors, all our disguises—soon washed away in the daily boiling ten-ton rain.

As I opened the cab's door, it croaked like a mating elephant.

"Señorita," the driver said in the way they all said it.

I leaned forward from the back seat and told him in English, "The Marines are going to love your sister."

The little light on the meter showed how he'd decorated the dash before him with silver A's and B's and C's, the paste-on type, arranged illiterately in crosses, swastikas, circles, and so on. "Where do you wish to go?" he answered in English.

"Honey-bunny, where do they all end up? The periodistas?" Although I was no longer officially a journalist.

"You wish the Inter-Continental."

THE TAXI smelled of locker rooms. The radio functioned, how unprecedented, and Radio Tempo was playing U.S. music, mostly: a non-stop mix of last season's Top 40 and last century's R&B hits . . . It was 1984, the real 1984, just before the elections would be postponed again; yet Radio Tempo concerned itself, in a city whose nightlife dribbled away to nothing by nine p.m., exclusively with bopping and dancing . . .

We travelled through the empty center of the capital, an

earthquake-leveled region where the enormous faces of several dead revolutionary leaders stared, looking iron-hard and Orwellian, out of their big billboard and across the bare fields toward the Mercado Central. The Mercado, a kind of shopping center, was closed and dark.

I tried to direct the driver the shortest way. But as usual I found it hard to talk, because I had no easy time of it even breathing, the diesel smoke was that thick, and the night's mugginess completed the impression that something with a head even more sizeable than these martyred Sandinistas', as to whose names I drew a blank, had taken Managua into its mouth . . .

And just let me say, while I'm on the subject, that trying to draw a decent breath of air in that place, especially downtown, fostered some appreciation of what it might be like to inhale a shirtsleeve soaked in horse-piss . . .

We dropped down toward the biggest hole in the city, actually a volcanic lake that had more or less surprised everybody with its presence one day, blessedly extinguishing the fiery torment of many hundreds. Now they had it set up as a kind of vast municipal swimming pool, offering refreshment to anybody sufficiently berserk to hike down into it; at the bottom there was a small bathhouse made out of hay, or something equally depressing, but in the dark the lake was a great gaping absence; and going up the hill away from it we passed on our left the Hospital Militar, and across the avenue from that the Sub-tenente's press office, Interpren, where they gave out the cards that said I was a journalist and not a whore.

We arrived.

The Inter-Continental Hotel in Managua goes up like a pyramid, somehow more white and pure with every floor, narrowing toward nothing, fewer rooms on each ascending storey . . .

And in the top penthouse, I suppose, is the Devil himself, inhaling the groans of the damned . . .

BECAUSE OF my unusual financial circumstances, I gave the cabdriver more money than he'd dreamed possible, and then pointedly, because I had to get strict with them, I cold-shouldered the boys and men out front of the hotel who washed cars and watched cars. Their chieftain sported as always his ridiculously shrunken Harley-Davidson tee-shirt. He spoke; I raised my middle finger in hatred. I wished I were dead, or at least more sensibly apparelled, if not swaddled in a death-shroud then at least dressed in flats and slacks—my ankles were tired and the backs of my knees itched with bug-bites . . .

By now they had me perfectly encoded at the Inter-Continental: as I approached the carpeted entrance, the door-man moved away from it . . . He actually stepped back, when he saw it was only me, and stood aside leaning on his little podium and looking right through my head as I pulled the door open for myself.

On the hotel's ground floor a concourse ran along a row of windows past shops and a buffet room toward the restaurant and the lounge. I made for the lounge.

Perhaps the doorman sensed my slipping descent in status, but the bartender was my kind of person, his features draped with the flag of bartending country, the veil of boredom.

"Your face escapes me," I told him, and asked for a martini.

He shook my drink to the tempo of our evening's entertainment, an overweight musical duo—that the only two fatsos in the whole zone had managed to find each other is one of those poignant miracles we were supplied with so abundantly here . . . One played the guitar, and the other didn't seem to do anything at all.

As the cabdriver had understood they would be, several journalists were drinking here tonight, the usual bunch, every one the sort of person who really ought to be shot dead right away.

The press gang had seized a couple of tables and were going at it now about how dull this election was.

I sat down with them a minute. They knew all about me, but what did they care? They'd come to this country to see the bullets fly. Tonight those of any account agreed Beirut was a much more interesting place than Managua, while the others who'd signed on forever down here passed no judgment.

A woman watching the elections for CBS, who'd run up north to the war a couple of times and only gotten rained on, was disappointed. "When I get back I'll see more action out front of La Guardia while I'm looking for a cab."

"You have to hustle," a man who obviously didn't like her said. "It's around. It's up there. But it's elusive—last week in Eslita they called an air strike down on some Contras a quarter mile from where I was standing. I got there in ten minutes with leaves in my fucking teeth, literally, from smashing along through the miserable brambles, and all I shot were holes in the ground. Meantime the bastards I'd been *with* had Contras up the ass—they'd got themselves ambushed exactly where I'd been standing."

I knew him, he'd lived down here for years, he really did work. He turned up here in front of a whiskey glass every third week, the rest of the time he slept in the jungle with the BLI, the elite—I doubted that—crack Brigada de Simón Bolívar, up in Matagalpa.

"There's no war. There are no Contras, there's no Matagalpa."

"No Honduras."

"I'd been so close, I almost expected to find I *had* some shots of the shit . . ."

Each one who did not have a vagina had a beard. All had cans of film bulging in their snap-flap pockets. They all drank as if they were just getting up to leave, but they never—I didn't blame them, believe me—got up and left unless forced.

"You have to hustle."

"Beirut."

"Right."

"You want bang-bang in Beirut, pull the film out of your pocket, wave it around . . ."

"Makes you thirsty just breathing the air."

"Gutters running with blood . . ."

"Lovely stuff."

"No such luck down here."

"The last man to get shot down here shot himself."

"We'll have to buy guns. We're going to have to shoot somebody ourselves."

"Arf-arf!"

"Moo! Moo!"

We began to snort and laugh. Smoke curled out of our ears. Our claws whined against the glass tabletop . . .

Word was the beer workers had gone on strike. We argued about whether a trip to the breweries would be worth anything at all.

Beer, along with meat, and toiletries, and cigarets, would soon be scarce. Beans were also in short supply. For months there'd been no milk. There were no replacements for burned-out bulbs or broken car parts.

When, in only minutes, I'd grown tired of us, I changed tables and sat down across from a possible European, a slack-witted Swede, I would have guessed, who was trying to negate this impression by wearing glasses.

By the time we'd introduced ourselves, his accent fairly placed him. I said, "And you're English?"

"Right you are. London, currently. And where are you from?"

"Here and there and yonder. What about yourself?"

"I—" He was a game sort. "Didn't we just do that one?"

I didn't answer.

Things got slow. I slipped off my heels and concentrated on cooling off, feet first.

Did he think I didn't see the glance pass between him and the barkeep?

I raised my glass to the martini expert. "Miguel. Alfonso. She's a little wet."

He didn't hear me.

"Smell the bamboo in here?" I asked the four-eyed Londoner.

"Oh, yes," he said. "Not quite a refreshing odor, is it?"

I said, "You have the kind of good manners that eventually get you killed."

Smiling neutrally, as if the music had perhaps mangled my words, he said, "Oh, my."

While Tweedledee and partner started a version of "Yesterday" in phonetically memorized English, I calculated that if I had the time right, this smelly lounge would be open another forty-five minutes. Long enough to get at least fractionally swacked before drifting into a taxi. Such was the scope of my thinking as I signalled for more and more booze. "Drier, hombre. Gin, sí, vermouth, no," I told the waiter.

My companion made himself cozy, folding his hands around his drink. "What brought you here?"

"I came on a plane."

He was embarrassed by my attitude and stared down into his glass.

"Yes. But I was wondering as to your motives," he began again.

He was what they call a pleasant enough man, meaning a giant nonentity . . . His features were pudding-like and ghostly, and in the center of this not-quite visage rested a pair of spectacles of the variety sported by Clark Kent and other such eunuchs . . . Except for the glasses, you couldn't remember his face even while staring straight into it.

"I can tell you my motives exactly. Have you ever had breakfast at the Sixty-third Street Y just off Broadway? New York?"

He shook his head.

"Well then, have you ever trapped something under a box? Brought a shoebox down over some little animal?"

He really wasn't listening.

"I wanted to know," I told him, "the exact dimensions of Hell."

He stirred his drink and wouldn't look anywhere but at his ice. "Are you for sale?"

So he'd heard all about me.

"I'm Press," I said.

"We're all Press," he said.

This was the only part that ever turned me on. "Then we're all for sale." I started to get warm between my legs.

He was smiling down at the table and appeared to be on the brink of vomiting. I felt sorry for him. He had to beg, he had to pay. Why do they always get you feeling sorry?

Because in truth there was nothing about him more lasting or substantial than your own glance reflected briefly in a window. You knew if he took those silly glasses off he'd disappear entirely from sight and mind, it would be as if he'd never existed, the waiter would clean his place without any comment and his hotel room would be rented out to some other stranger with a blank space in his passport where there was supposed to be a photo . . .

Merely to confuse him I told him the truth: "I came here to be a contact person for Eyes for Peace up north in Matagalpa. In the town of Aswalil."

"Oh, really," he said, "Aswalil, that's one of the rougher spots, I understand."

"In a sense," I said.

"Well, is it? I mean what made you decide to leave, for instance?"

"What made me think I'd last in the Girl Scouts any longer than I lasted—two and a half days?" One more drink and I was out of here. The guy was deeply homosexual, in all likelihood a castrato of some sort. "It's not the Contras, honey, it's the garbage. Breakfast-lunch-and-dinner, eating fruit that drips all over you with your feet in the dirt."

"Oh. I see," he said without assurance.

"Not that Manhattan was any better," I admitted, "I mean, riding through life with a parking ticket clamped between my teeth . . ."

"Ah," he said, "I, uh—" et cetera.

Finally, after having held off all day, the rain started outside.

Nowhere on Earth is there an automatic carwash quite as zany as one of these storms. We could hear it·through the closed windows, moving sideways against every structure like an assault of razors.

"And you are here for what," I asked in order to appear polite.

"With the Watts people," he said. "I say with, but of course I mean alone."

"The Watts people. The oil company."

"Right. In a charitable cause, I suppose you might say."

"Please don't go into detail, babe."

"Well, how many companies, at this moment, would consider investing here?"

"Not many, I'd imagine." Not enough to form a bowling league, or hadn't Watts Petroleum heard?

"Right you are again." He was happy with himself. "All right, of course it's all in the name of profit, but it has, let's say, humanitarian overtones, the mere idea of throwing business their way."

A humanitarian in Hell—worse even than my own observer-punishment! His life must have been marked by more than several bad crimes. This guy, at some point in his earthly existence, must have been truly evil, possibly Hitlerian.

I'd have demanded his autograph, but what was the point? We can't remember our sins here. We don't know who we used to be.

"Now that we understand each other," I said, "what about some supper?"

"Oh, well, isn't it kind of late?"

"Lunch then."

"That's much more reasonable."

There was something about him I liked. "You make me sick. For a price I'll sleep with you," I told him.

MAKING LOVE with him was like passing through a patch of fog . . .

He was a pale and faintly freckled person, with that sort of flesh that bruises at a touch . . .

WHEN HE was finished he sat up and put his hand on his pants, which were draped over the telephone on the nightstand, as if he wanted to grab them and go, run off, jump out the window. But it was his room.

I told him I wanted to be paid in dollars.

"Everybody wants dollars, don't they," he said.

It's a rule I have never to say anything further on the subject of my wishes after stating them to a jay-naked customer, because they get you talking, and pretty soon you relent.

He turned on the bedside lamp. "Well then," he said, picking two twenties and a ten out of his wallet in the jarring, interrogator's glare. "And you're quite right, too. There's talk they're going to roll up the currency."

It was bright as a flashbulb in the room. I felt as naked as I was. "Roll up?"

"Yah."

"Roll up . . ."

"Run down some of the black-market stuff. Call in the foreigners and check their dollar supply, and so on. Us foreigners. Our dollar supplies."

"Fuck *me*."

"And—would I have to pay extra for it?" He put out the lamp, and then cut back the sudden blindness with his lighter while he got a cigaret going.

"Check their dollar supply."

"Right."

"I have no dollar supply. I live entirely on black-market cordobas."

Wordlessly he smoked in the darkness . . .

"You don't have to start thinking how to ditch me," I told him. "I'm not after your dollars. I'm here for the air-conditioning."

I stood by the window, where the cooling unit's breath could find my armpits.

Things weren't perfect. But this was quite the recipe for soothing financial anxiety—U.S. money, cool room, quiet night, moonlight down through the venetian blinds, and the blue hair of his cigaret smoke drifting in the slats of light . . .

"You're thinking so hard how to ditch me your head is smoking," I told him, "what do you think of that?"

"I'm thinking something quite a bit different," he said . . . Faceless voice in a dark bedroom somewhere . . . "What I'm thinking is that I could very easily stroll right out of myself. This isn't the first time I've committed adultery. I do it quite often. But I can't stand it . . ." His face bloomed behind the glow of his cigaret . . . "I don't really miss anybody . . . I feel I'm in danger of throwing my life away . . ."

"You're not moving. You're not in danger."

"I'm not moving," he said. "I'm not in danger."

Now I heard the adrenaline running out of his voice. He'd probably just stepped off a fifteen-hour flight.

"I came here to be generous," he was saying in a flat tone, "but there's a chance I've overstepped. Perhaps I've given away too much."

"It's late, darling," I said, "let's not start hauling out the snapshots of the family."

"Of course. I'm being messy."

He was a mess, all right. It was a wonder I hadn't spotted it right off. But they're all a little demented away from home.

He offered me a cigaret—a filter, as I discovered on accepting it, from Costa Rica. Filter brands were rare lately in Managua. "Derby," I told him, quoting the sharks who manufactured these lung-scrapers, "es el cigarrillo. Thanks."

Before I knew it I was asleep, and I trust he took that as the highest compliment . . . After all, you can't sleep in the same bed with all that many of them—a few you wouldn't want to shut your eyes, even briefly, in their presence. But I woke up in the night and he was out of bed, standing by the window. I was lost. It was the kind of moment that beats with a sinister heart. The air-conditioner hummed raggedly and the whole building seemed to have erased itself, along with everything else. Leaving him, me, and this black dislocated room . . .

And then I heard some drunken reporters upstairs arguing in German or whatever and smashing a bottle, and I felt the world again and saw that this guy was probably not too horrible, just another foreign businessman, the dregs of his company's executive work force, or he wouldn't be here, would he —just another confused person with a briefcase and a poor report to bring back.

I don't know how he guessed I was awake. "Shall we meet again?" he asked me.

"Again and again. Anytime you've got fifty U.S."

"Yes," he said. "Of course . . ."

Oh, I felt bad . . . I liked his style. I enjoyed his company. But please, actually I'm not in the habit of taking an emotional bed-check in my dark heart each time some libidinally impoverished lackey of pig billionaires gets the wrong idea. Or what if it was the right idea? In any case it was an idea entirely his own, wasn't it, and let him stagger around his rented bedroom holding his head. At that moment I had to get a little rest . . . How fast the tropics sap you . . .

I COULD walk through hours like doorways in the middle of the night, if only the middle of the night would last for hours—midnight's the only time a somber if not exactly a reverent breath blows along the air of Managua—holding in my head a few lines from one of the great poets of the Inferno, William S. Merwin. I can turn onto one of these rackety lanes cobbled with mashed fruit and urchin-dung and hear, honestly hear out loud, William Something Merwin saying *I have seen streets where the hands of the beggars / Are left out at night like shoes in a hotel corridor* . . .

Of course, the streets aren't literally like that here, they aren't lined, I mean to say, with whacked-off appendages, but the hotel corridors are, I've left the Inter-Continental in the very small hours with someone else's money in my purse and seen the hands laid out by the doors, and the lost voices hung on wooden pegs behind the doorman's podium, and the tongue-cut bellboys delivering potions and poisons along the halls. And I've stepped out under the awning, and across the small parking lot where the taxis usually stand I've seen men in white robes and hoods conspiring together, and the haunted Negro singer Robert Johnson swinging from a rope by his broken neck.

They left him there for days, and eventually the rope lengthened so that his feet, in blue tennis shoes, were flat on the dirt; he seemed to be standing there with his neck in a noose and his chin on his shoulder, thinking.

A guy who's been strung-up drops down gradually on his rope like a slow-motion spider. The rope stretches. Pretty soon he's standing around on the ground just like the rest of us, only he's deceased, grey-blue, textured like a sausage, and undergoing his putrefaction at a rapid clip in this sweltering mush of a climate. You can't even see the rope around his neck because it bites in, and the flesh swells up around it, the flesh incorporates the very instrument of its demise . . .

Or maybe this is a twisted memory of a hanging I saw in Matagalpa . . .

But whatever had happened in Matagalpa was already the discredited past. Impossible to prove. And it explains nothing. Nothing explains why I did what I did . . .

But I'm saying that I was in the habit of walking the midnights after work, barefoot, dangling a high-heeled shoe from either hand, in the only hour when the temperature was bearable. Morning's an oven; noon is a star; dusk is a furnace; but the middle of the night, at its worst, is only a hot bath . . . I always took a meandering route between the front door of the Inter-Continental, or the Tico, another place I trolled nearer the capital's outskirts, and the dead-end dirt lane where I lived. I usually got in about four a.m. and sat listening to Radio Tempo in the sort of lobby of La Whatsis, the sort of motel I stayed in. I forget the name of this wonderful motel. I only know it wasn't the Inter-Continental. In the lobby there was a desk, a padlocked telephone, a ratty couch oftentimes draped with somebody's wildly snoring cousin or uncle, and a hi-fi of which the radio, at least, worked. Six rooms, all in a row; and at the end of the hall, a door beyond which lay a vast roofed area where half of Managua, it seemed, resided in casual squalor. They washed the towels and sheets back there, brewed up for themselves simmering meals of slop, raised their degenerate offspring, chased away dogs the whites of whose eyes were forever showing. It was going on all over this section of Managua, in a series of dirt yards pocked by lives.

And me? I was much better off than most, living in a room with a concave double bed, a desk that aspired to become an orange crate, a broken air-conditioner, a cloying damp that seemed to originate in the shower stall . . . There was a toilet, too, and a single faucet overlooking a big white bowl.

On one wall was an unframed inspirational poster, a close-up view of one of the wounded, bleeding hands of Jesus, actually, with clouds and saints and mourners drifting in colorful dolor all around it. And I was supplied with one other picture also, next to that one, of bulldogs in human dress smoking cigars and shooting pool.

As soon as the first drop of dawn dilutes the blackness, the neighbors begin their unbelievable racket, first the roosters, then the radios, then the live accompaniment to the radios— and then it's time to wind up the little children and start their screams and tears—and finally with the pots and pans . . . The yard's enclosed by a rusty corrugated fence, but the fence has, in addition to countless bullet-holes, many long ragged gashes in it, and anytime after daylight you'll find crazed dogs, dust-covered urchins, old crones draped in black, or people who've slipped their chains—this morning it's an auburn-haired little girl in a dress, also auburn; and her tiny nude brother—maneuvering among the puddles that soak the grass under the only tree, hoping for something they can try their teeth on, perhaps clots of dirt. Their perseverance is astonishing. Naturally, as an observer-tormentee, I have to watch. It's one of the refinements of my punishment here that I'm forced to appreciate the little boy's pinched buttocks, and the rivulets of dust where the pee is drying down the left thigh beneath his uncircumcised carroty little penis, and the nature of his older sister's ankles, which seemed designed expressly for flat-footed squatting in unconscious misery on the earth.

I keep the good word close to hand like a ticket. / *I feed the wounded lights in their cages,* says William Something Merwin somewhere. It's a miracle, another miracle, that the wounded maintain their appetites at *all* living in an odor of rotten grass and a smell I've always associated with things canine, yet one more miracle in the supurating glue of miracles hereabouts, oh and the monkey-man who churns the vat of it appreciates, I'm sure, that the voltage of slight hunger in my own stomach turns maximum because I know that unlike these dirty, awful children, I'll get breakfast.

Understandably I hated this neighborhood . . . But I would never get into a place like the Inter-Continental or the Tico on my own steam—and I couldn't hop a plane and disappear, either. Because I didn't have dollars.

The truth is, I'd suddenly, in a panic of avarice, turned all my dollars into an airline bag full of black-market cordobas at one-twentieth the official rate in La Cruz, Costa Rica, the last town before the Nicaraguan border; and had crossed over with tens of thousands of them in my underwear—hidden and smuggled like that because the Sandinistas know those Contra families are out there selling their exiled worthless cash at whatever price they can get: there's a limit on the number of cordobas you can bring in. A limit that I ignored, as I say, and so I came over rich—but even the Nicaraguans themselves don't want their internationally laughed-at currency coming across the counters at them when they suspect there's a U.S. dollar to be had. Therefore the rule is that if you carry Caesar's passport, you pay with Caesar's coin: the greenback. I didn't have any.

Up in the northern provinces, they hadn't cared so much that I had only cordobas, but down here in the capital they wanted what they said they wanted—U.S., U.S.—and I didn't have it. I was black market.

What's why I was cornered in a room at the Whatsis Motel, with the breakfast-hour floor show of naked children starving . . .

That's why no photographer would take me north where the stories were, not even the French photographers who didn't care about anything but bang-bang, a phrase that does not refer to sex but the noises of war: they didn't want me continually impeding their hustle with my bagful of jive money . . .

That's why Sub-tenente Whoever had me in a hammer-lock, so that he or any bureaucrat of his acquaintance could lift my press card, or my skirts, pretty much whenever the mood clouted him, and *chinga* me . . .

Instead of the descent of sleep I now felt a familiar panic . . . A visitation of tropical claustrophobia . . . Sailing rudderless into the day just made everything so much worse, but it wasn't rare for me to run as if on fire into the streets in the morning, it was getting, in fact, to be a cyclical thing, like a searing comet—best combatted by a little squeeze, a few drops of rum.

Two fingers of the stuff, all I had, didn't work. I let the bottle roll away and jumped up and dressed, raving out loud at everybody keeping me down, and headed through the lobby convinced I had to get out of this toilet *today* . . . Knowing I was fated never to get out—not in this life, not in this death . . .

W I T H   I T S loud diesel engines and unmuffled motor-cycles, its choking fumes and loud cries, Managua is like New York City in summer—Manhattan, in a sense, is a

Third World nation—although the only Managuan building fat as a New York one is TELCOR.

TELCOR is where I was going. TELCOR meant words with the world above.

Here and there in this country there were telephones, but if one wanted to call Planet Earth, one put the call through at TELCOR, the small, timeless, dead center of Hell, where souls were being branded with the shapes of their hope . . . As soon as you enter you go deaf—there can be no voice to these cries . . . If you bring a camera, the film exposes itself on entering . . . The minutes stop, but the ticking gets louder . . . People blow their noses and cough . . . The green fire of boredom streaks the air . . . The children on their mothers' laps seem to drip with pain . . . Nothing happens, you never get out, and it all just gets worse and worse forever . . . Imagine a bus station presided over by demons, some of them hateful and some of them helpful, where the buses never come . . . A doctor's anteroom but the doctor is dead . . . Eventually they call a name that sounds like yours and shout the number of the booth they expect you to enter, and either you get one without a door, so that everybody waiting to make whatever calls the burning circumstances are forcing them to make can now memorize the names of your contacts and trace the character of your desires, or you close yourself up behind the Plexiglas while the chamber fills with your used breath until you really can just no longer speak.

First you have to fight your way to the front of the crowd, and pay. I estimated the length of my call: "Five minutes."

"You will pay in dollars," the little man behind the counter said.

For a moment I simply floated on my oceanic resentment of that one. "It's customary that I pay in cordobas," I said, pronouncing the Spanish phrases the best I could. "It's customary."

Beside me and on top of me and underneath me before this counter, as if we'd all been bulldozed up against it, were dozens of other people trying to get their messages across.

"Your passport," the little man said.

Passport was always the final word in this argument. I paid in dollars—day rates; fifteen bucks!—and stood waiting beneath the high clock in the room of tears.

This is a small chamber in a big building—out the door is a monstrous ground-floor, marbly, resonant, like Grand Central Station. Towering murals depicting the red-scarved heroes of the revolution prove that this administration's been around long enough, at least, to affect the decor. Soldiers with their Chinese AK-47's slung barrel-down march back and forth—they were just little boys when first handed those weapons, but they've grown with the revolution, now they're older and steadier, sometime soon they'll start shaving . . .

Was I calling somebody for money, or what? By the time I was actually summoned to my booth, I'd forgotten what it was all about . . . But, of course, I was a journalist, I was calling my editor . . . There was a crepitation in the earpiece, his voice, supposedly . . .

Soon we were quarrelling.

"Louder," I told him, "slower, I can't quite—"

"Why would a collegiate fashion magazine be interested in anything, any person, any event, in the fucking *continent* of *Nicaragua?*"

"Your geography is a little loose, there. I'm saying I can get you a wonderful piece on San José, Costa *Rica . . .*"

"Is this the same routine as last time? Is this Telex me X amount of cash and never hear from me ever in your life again?"

"You're hearing from me *now.* Just get me to San José and I'll get organized. Things aren't as simple as you want to think."

"Does this sound simple, fuck you? Does fuck you sound simple enough?"

"Please bear in mind that I am employed by you."

"Are you on drugs, honey? You are not, and never have been, employed by me. Never never."

"Just what are you trying to say?"

"Something along the lines of what I just said, darling."

"I have a press card right here in my—in my stupid, sweaty purse—wait a minute—"

"You sound great, Managua, let's get together *soonest*, and have lunch—"

"*Wait* a minute—it says *Roundup Magazine*—"

"Bye-bye, Señorita." Click. Clackety—whack buzz hum—nothing's uncomplicated this morning in Centroamerica, not the phone calls, not the phones, not the mechanical expletives of the phones . . . Half a dozen terrorists were gesturing helpfully that I should now replace the receiver on its hook. "Señorita . . . Señorita . . ."

For a long time I had felt the matter of me shrinking to where I was known only as the last place: they'd say, "Hello, New York," and start glancing through the bad checks, "Hello, Spokane," and go for the buzzer . . . These days I was down to nowhere, to nothing, now I was down to Señorita . . .

Home! New York! Goddamn it! The smug Judases! The lying hypocrites, et cetera—around me were people whose lies were at least desperate and unabashed. Of course, I'd been the one lying the most over the phone . . . But the other party had been evasive! shady! unwholesome! . . .

And now, cretinously mumbling, a young sentry blocked my way out the door.

"Por favor, motherfucker, hable más despacio," I said. Not that even abject pleading ever got them to talk any slower.

"You have to use the other door," he said.

And them too! Don't forget them! Pay in dollars! Use the

other door! As if this one didn't work, wasn't wide open! Goddamn them also! . . . I longed for the sight of U.S. tanks further chewing up the streets of this slovenly capital where it was possible only to get nothing done and nobody seemed to think nothing not enough . . .

Down here, the sight of a lady weeping crazily in front of a big public building warms everybody's heart. They smile at me as they pass . . . "Taxi!"—I scream it like an oath, and the whole capital screeches to a halt: in the Inferno, 1984, anything that moves is for hire . . .

I SPEND the rest of the morning battening down at a patio restaurant across the main road from the Inter-Continental: Los Paraquitos, I suppose it's called . . . Incarcerated birds are their trademark . . . The sound system plays Spanish-language versions of "Under the Boardwalk" and "By the Time I Get to Phoenix." I'm out of the sun; the breeze across the flagstones is not hot enough to ignite my clothing. This little corner of the game opens for business at ten, but I'm the only living thing on the patio at this hour, aside from four parrots in a big cage.

To the extent that I wear skirts and cheap nylon slips, I've gone native. But it doesn't take long to find me out. Already the waiter realizes I don't have much Spanish. Out of respect for my homeland, the waiter's bringing me ketchup and mustard . . . He gives me a vast, four-page menu of which, he explains, one meat item is actually available; one vegetarian; several fish.

"Rum," I say. Never any shortage of that.

Several soldiers passed along the low hedge beside me and crossed the street, all of them, in the macho manner, without looking right or left. Didn't they ever get knocked down?

Would such people really come banging at my door to count my cordobas and arrest me? Was there honestly an investigation?

Oh, what was I panicking for?—as reason returned with a drop of Tres Ríos rum and a minute in the shade . . . I had thirty-five U.S. dollars, in most circles a phenomenal stash. If I spent only cordobas today, and found a customer to pay in dollars tonight, I'd have enough money for the five p.m. Aeronica out of here tomorrow.

If I hesitated, if I spent my dollars, I'd have to ride a bus to Liberia in Costa Rica, and that would take ten hours on post-revolutionary Nicaragua's decimated section of the Pan-american Highway . . . Diesel and dust—sweat, rain, and wet straw. The children along there are streaked with dried mud. Their hair is in knots. They don't seem to have any parents. Or so much as a prayer—the small Catholic church this side of the southern border crossing is closed, padlocked, all boarded up, I know that much . . . I went out back of it, the day I came across, to squat down daintily over the crawling flowers and relieve myself.

I crossed the frontier from Costa Rica in the south, down from the cool hills, through the soggy checkpoints, and right into the factory of bugs in the towering grass this side of the border, bugs raining down through the air, a perpetual cloud of them overshadowing the Lago de Nicaragua so that they cake, absolutely *putty*—I'm talking about *bugs*—all these leprous diesel-spewing vehicles trying to crawl through the choking deluge . . . I don't know at what point, maybe it's as you pass the second or third miserable sugar refinery looking just like a prison, that you realize you've been ejected from Paradise. And whatever these stunned, drenched people did to get themselves banished here is an absolute mystery. Like your own mortal error . . . Because, after all, the damned don't arrive carrying the memories of their fat black sins in their heads, you don't think of yourself as taking up your citizenship in Hell, nobody expects to cross the border and immediately start licking dirt like a snake—I myself would have perpetrated suicide at Checkpoint One if I'd imagined I'd come here as anything but an observer. But to observe is my designated agony, the sharpest punishment is just to *watch* . . . While being treated always and everywhere, incidentally, like a sucker—ripped-off—laughed at—exposed and hated— forced to show the midnight-blue passport like a stain on my hands . . .

All the authorities are dead . . . Or in any case they no longer, and no longer do even their ghosts, inhabit the embassies . . . The community swims in the water of earthquake craters . . .

And I am getting out of here.

And as I enjoy the peristaltic quiver each icy sip of rum produces, I believe I witness my salvation . . .

It's the bespectacled Londoner of last night, looking over the parrots as if this were a zoo. But he isn't interested so much in these enormous flashy birds as in the parking lot beyond their cage and on the other side of the patio's hedge of oleander, through which he's peering.

THERE WAS something princely about him . . . In his cool, cerulean blue suit, his skin so clean and pink in the scorching daylight . . . What if my heart moved? What if I went for him at that moment? So what?

I felt stung that he didn't notice me. After all, I was the only other human this side of the kitchen—no, the big oil executive was now joined by the gentleman he'd been peeking at, who came onto the patio from the parking lot and greeted him quietly, one of the Nicaraguans that Watts Petroleum had business with, I supposed—one of the endless train of Nicaraguans in green sunglasses and white shirts, if Watts represented possible profit—here to mooch lunch or receive a bribe.

I S A W the man from England in his blue suit again at supper, sitting with the same official, or another official just like that one, in the restaurant at the Inter-Continental.

As I came in, I nodded to the Englishman. But he ignored me.

I was very embarrassed and pretended to look over the buffet while thinking of a reason to leave.

I was sick of eating here . . . Well, but it was the only outfit in the region capable of putting on a buffet, and they allowed me to pay with my black-market cordobas. The lunch buffets, held in a much larger room, were extravagant, accompanied by live piano, buzzing with journalists and other international crooks and phonies. I wondered why none of them ever ate supper here . . . Probably because it was the most expensive place in the country.

I stole a glance. My British friend looked much less the sovereign—suddenly he was hung over, pale, and shaken. He was all alone now, his meal pushed aside.

"Hello," I said to him like a fool, "has your dinner guest ducked out, or what, exactly?"

I felt like changing his face with a fork when he stared at me as if I were a total stranger.

"Well, excuse my ass all to hell," I said to him.

His mouth stayed shut. I retreated temporarily. Time to use the washroom downstairs here at the Inter-Continental, where yesterday, at any rate, they'd had toilet paper. And I had to steal some for my room at the Motel Whatsis.

The Englishman's companion, I noticed, was now sitting in one of the wicker chairs on the promenade reading somebody's discarded *La Prensa*. And you too, I thought. You too.

At my motel, we got neatly defined squares of newsprint. The ladies' room at the Inter-Continental offered a pinkish brand of toilet paper this evening—the first color other than paper-bag brown I'd seen in Centroamerica. I unhooked a roll from its receptacle and put it in my purse.

Tonight's graffiti read:

> RED, *white and blue*
> *I shit on you!*

> V*iva*
> R*eagan-muerto*

> "*If they*
> *move, kill 'em!*"
> W*illiam Holden—The Wild Bunch*

Back in the restaurant, the rude British man from the Watts Oil Corporation found me as I looked over the dinner selection, which appeared, for some reason, to be more like breakfast.

He said, "I had a reason for ignoring you, believe it or not."

"It's okay. Whatever my true feelings."

"I'm sorry," he said. "It's the man I was with, you see. He's gone now. I was afraid he was coming back."

"Consorting with unescorted women is no disgrace down here," I told the poor man. "Latins think it's normal."

"No . . ."

While I got myself some supper, moving from dish to dish, he moved beside me. "I was concerned for *your*—for your reputation, believe it or not. That is—oh, for goodness' sake, what have I said—forgive me, will you?"

He was upset. He mopped his face with a bare hand. His napkin was hanging out of his belt.

"Who *is* that friend of yours? What did he do to you?"

The Englishman waved his hand, as if trying to cancel our conversation with this gesture. I pulled him into a booth right next to the buffet.

"He's still here. He's sitting out there on the promenade," I said.

"Oh God."

"He's reading the paper."

"I see."

"Who is he?" I said.

"A Costa Rican. He claims to represent the OIJ."

I pronounced it for him: "The Oh-Ee-Hota."

"He called it the Oh, Eye, Jay."

"For you, huh? For your Anglo ears. Oh, Ee,—'jota' is our 'j,' see."

"Gotcha," he said with some irritation.

"Those are the Costa Rican cops," I said.

"Yes, the Costa Rican, that's the spy . . . Actually it's quite a good—a large detective force," he said.

"What have you got to do with them? Or don't I want to know?"

"Oh . . . Well . . ." he said miserably.

"I don't want to know."

He shook his head.

"You need a drink."

"No, no. Thanks. A cup of tea. I've got one . . ."

He brought his tea over from his table; and we sat there silently at mine while he suffered right in my face and I tried to eat. Weren't we all in some kind of a jam down here? The important thing was we weren't wasting away, we weren't combing the dirt for bits of old bone to chew . . .

No, my coffee was being poured at this moment by a waiter in a chartreuse vest . . . Scrambled eggs and fried potatoes. Yards of white tablecloth, cups of flame beneath the steel warming-pans, mounds of crushed ice in which were bedded down sliced pineapple and three or four kinds of melon, and there was even some reconstituted milk—God alone knew what crimes lay back of its delivery—in a tall stainless-steel pitcher bathed in a cold sweat . . .

He said, "It seems I've ventured beyond the bounds of reasonable conduct."

"I like the way you talk," I told him. "You're so hopelessly fucking out of it."

"Out of it," he said, stirring the milk into his tea. "I'm beginning to think that's precisely the case."

"Are you familiar with the American expression 'You've got your ass in a sling'?"

"I'm familiar with most of your expressions." He placed his hands before him on the tablecloth. "I'm familiar with a lot of things. I'm familiar with many of the capitals of the world. And if you don't mind, I'm familiar with whores. I'm familiar with the way whores try desperately to act as if they feel superior to those of us who pay them. When actually you feel quite inferior. When actually you feel ashamed. Why didn't you look at our waiter when he talked to you? Why don't you look at me when I'm saying something?"

"Because there's nothing to see."

"Then why do you avoid my gaze, if I'm nobody at all to you?"

"Can we back this up a little? Because, actually, I'm not the one the OIJ is scaring shitless down at the Inter-Continental. Am I."

That relaxed him some, at least with respect to his inventory of my failings. "No," he said. "I'm the one."

"Your ass is in a sling. You've got your tit caught in a wringer."

"I'm all in a muddle," he agreed.

"Well, you've still got your sense of humor."

"You're very kind. I owe you an apology, a whole group of them, rather. I only said those things because I'm so nervous. 'Frightened' is a better word."

"Not at all," I assured him.

But I would never forgive him for talking to me that way.

"You're very kind," he said. "And I'm very nervous."

"Whatever it is, can it really be all that bad?"

"I don't see how it could be worse," he said.

"Why? What on earth did you do?"

"Somewhat in the nature of—I'd say it was a mix between —I passed along the secrets of a company to the secret-gatherers of a government. That's mixing industrial and international espionage, I'd say."

"And you're caught."

He grappled in his shirt pocket for his Derbys—not just the fingers, but the whole arm trembled so you worried, would he behave all right—really, it was terrible to watch. "We've already agreed my ass is in a sling."

"Can I have one of those Derbys, please?" I said.

He had a nice lighter.

I used this lighter and held it in my hand and said, "So why didn't the Oh-Ee-Hota roll you up just now?"

"He is not—the OIJ have nothing to do with this. It's complicated. The question of jurisdiction is a little involved."

"Well, yes, really. Maybe he doesn't know he's a long way from Costa Rica. Why don't we find a soldier and get him arrested?"

"Because I'm so very out of my depth," he said, "so out of it, I admit it . . . I have no idea yet whose side the OIJ are on. Or even whose side I'm on. That man may be the only friend I've got."

"Does he say he's your friend?"

"Yes, he does."

"Then never talk to him again. Did he say his name?"

"He showed me his identity cards and a badge."

"Don't talk to him anymore. Forget him. Do you have a gun? Shoot him."

"*I* don't have a *gun.*" He was panicking again. "I'm honestly just a—*stupid* Senior Analyst, research and development, Watts Petroleum Corporation, and that is all. That is all."

"Let's lose this man."

"I've only been Senior for one month."

"Heartrending. Let's ditch him down at the Mercado Central. I'll pick you up in a cab, see, in a spot where he can't get one. We'll leave him standing there."

"He happens to drive a car. What about his car?"

"He parks his car, follows you to the other end of the Mercado, and there I am, waiting for you in a cab—are you following this idea? By the time he gets back to his car, we're long gone."

"Then what?"

"I can't line all that up for you. The Mercado idea sounds like a hit, is all."

"I believe you're drunk."

All too true. "Would I be sitting here if I was the littlest bit sober? No," I said. "No."

"I don't have any objection to leaving," he said. "But the business of getting away from this man is just silly."

"You can't trust anybody down here. I was going to steal this," I confessed. I handed him back his cigaret lighter.

"Were you really," he said as if he hadn't heard me at all.

ON THE way out we passed right by the OIJ man. He'd rolled up his copy of *La Prensa*, and he tapped it against his knee as he sat in his chair on the promenade, his sunglasses cocked on his head, watching us approach and watching us recede.

The Britisher seemed compelled to offer him something beyond dumb acknowledgment. "I, oh, uh," he began.

I pulled him along. "You don't have to explain anything to that person," I said.

By the time we were off and running in a taxi, an old wrinkled Ford driven very slowly by an old wrinkled man, the Costa Rican was pulling out behind us in a four-wheel-drive Daihatsu, one of those Asian makes you never hear of outside the Third World . . .

"That's him back there," I told the Englishman.

"I wouldn't know. Don't look. My God, it's a *tank*. He told me he had a car."

"That's him. He's got Costa Rican plates, too. They look like the new California plates, you know?"

"No," he said, "I didn't know that."

"Will you go very much faster, please?" I asked the driver.

"No."

"One of the few on Earth," I noted.

"We can't expect to lose him driving as slow as this," the Englishman said.

"We're going to get rid of him down at the Mercado," I reminded him.

"What's the point? He'll only wait back at my hotel."

The rain started: they might have been letting down a truckload of marbles on the roof . . .

We rolled up the windows and commenced suffocating. "This is impressive," my friend said. "The wipers are useless. Can he see?"

"Can you see?" I asked the driver.

"No."

"Is he still back there?"

"I can't see a thing," I said.

We were crawling. Soon the rain lessened by half, and things were visible again, but now our driver was held up by one muddy pond after another that had laid itself down across the road.

We were driving past the FSLN campaign headquarters. For the benefit of the new arrival I pointed it out, a circular building set by itself at the border of the huge wiped-out central area, rippling behind sheets of rain.

"It's big, isn't it," he said.

"Well, I guess the Frente has all the money."

"The campaign offices for the other parties aren't quite as impressive, you're saying."

"No way. I don't even know where the others are—no, wait, I've seen the MPL or whatever, the Communists. They've got a big chain-link fence, and a lot of rifles waving around out front. But that's their whole general center of operations—not just a campaign outfit."

"So the Sandinistas are going to win."

"Win what?

"Well . . ." He was confused. "The election."

"If there's an election in this country, babe, don't blink—or you'll miss the whole show."

"But the elections are scheduled," he said. "The elections are going to take place."

"They're not going to let anybody vote. They'll postpone it again. And they'll blame the U.S."

"I don't believe you."

"Why would they risk losing? Why would they let go of all the power once they had it?"

"Because they believe in principles. Because those principles would grow *stronger* if they chanced losing that power in the name—if they played fair in the name," he said, "of certain principles."

"Like what principles? Let's hear these names."

"Equality, democracy."

"Liberty, fraternity, right, yeah, right."

"Why am I talking to you?" he said bitterly.

"Yerbabuena," I told the cabdriver.

"El Mercado," the driver corrected me.

"No, let's go to the Yerbabuena now instead," I said. "I'll show you some liberty and some of that other bullshit," I told the British customer.

THE CAB driver wanted fifty. I gave him a hundred. "Wait for us," I said. He nodded, turned off the engine, and sank into his seat to outlast the rain in a stupor, as we intended to do in the Yerbabuena, Managua's rip-off socialist bookstore.

However slimy its impostures, the Yerbabuena had the most air-conditioned air in town and was more like home than any other place I'd seen since stepping off the plane a year ago in the capital of Costa Rica. The Yerbabuena had the sweetened rusticity—shelves of clean yellow wood with a satin finish, lots of light, coffee and cakes for sale, and solid manly wooden tables to sit at—of Big Sur, California. But unlike Big Sur this place had pretentious waiters in cheap wine-red jackets. Only disenfranchised intellectuals and left-tourists came here. With that tentativeness of foreigners, people stood in front of the shelves reading the spines of the books.

Aside from pastry and coffee there were propagandistic tee-shirts for sale at 1,500—at the official rate, that was over fifty bucks—and soft-cover books printed on weightless paper: tracts, rationalizations, biographies, whitewashcs, smears, like *La Muerte de Sandino*, the sad testimonial account of Somoza's murder of the rebel.

We found a table by the window, looking out at the beautiful taxicab we'd arrived in and, two car-lengths down the curb, our cop's hulking jeep.

The proprietress of the Yerbabuena, draped all over with jewelry, sat near the cake selection going over the ledger, it appeared—a hard-case capitalist ritzily coping through a whole deck of regimes. I hated her fat, red lips . . . When I complained about her in a low voice, the Watts Corporation's Senior and soon to be ex-Analyst said, "And what do you believe in?"

"I'm just keeping my head above the flood. At least I'm not in it entirely for profit."

"You believe in survival."

"Are you going to help me sort out my beliefs now? I just wanted you to see this place."

"It's pleasant."

"It's a little piece of Palo Alto. A little piece of Cambridge."

"England?"

"Boston."

"And Palo Alto?"

"California. If we wanted Disneyland, they'd serve up some of that. They're just patiently taking our cash and trying to keep the Marines away."

He made no comment. The waiter came, and we ordered

coffee. "Why are you looking at us like that?" I asked the waiter. That put a stop to his act. "Snotty," I told him in English.

"And what about you?" I asked the Londoner. "Are you a believer? Is there a reason for everything that happens?"

Exhausted and despairing, he didn't answer.

But in such dry, cool air you can't help but feel, before long, the hope returning. We had coffee. The rain stopped, and the last drops blew out of the air. The sun came back, mist rose from the pavements. We didn't wonder how we'd started for the Mercado and ended here. It made sense to sit in the air-conditioned Harvard-style bookstore and watch the rain dry first off the concrete lampposts and then, starting from the tops, off the hides of the streetside palm trees. Each tree and post had got wet along one side only.

The waiter was, unfortunately, a debilitated gelding. He wouldn't come around when I wanted more coffee. I struggled in Spanish with some of the more insulting idioms. This brought over the proprietress. I must have been soggy with rum and taxi rides, because although there was only one of her, she appeared to triangulate and converge.

"It's bad the way you talk to my waiter," she said, then more, but I couldn't follow her Spanish.

"He's rude. He's the son of his daddy," I said, meaning he was spoiled.

"You've done it two times," she went on. "Once before, and now today."

"I've never visited your shop before." I wished it were true.

She said no more but went over to the waiter and said softly, "Lying." The waiter was released from his delicacies. He delivered the check at once and, preliminary to screwing me for dollars, asked what country I was from: "Tu país?" The fop, the choirboy.

I pointed at the Englishman. "Maybe he wears a toupee. I don't."

This broke the Englishman up. His mirthful outburst was a shock, a regular string of firecrackers. It continued in fits. In his eyes there was nothing funny, but he couldn't stop. He looked around, confused and nearly purple in the face, trying to stifle himself.

I yanked out a few dozen cordobas for the waiter . . . The patrons around us looked on blankly . . . Bad money, the police, rancid motel, stupid taxi . . . Now this moment . . . It was all too much . . . We left in defeat, the Englishman belatedly disguising his hysteria as a bad coughing episode. On the post-revolutionary street, on a street that had seen gun battles, the sight of one person helping another bent-over raised a peculiar alertness in some boys leaning against a stack of tires in a garage . . . Our cabbie looked away . . . The OIJ man, behind the wheel of his Daihatsu, was suddenly sitting straight up and peering at us . . .

"Now the Mercado," I told our driver. The old man made a blind, macho-hombre U-turn. Meanwhile, having wiped his nose and eyes, the Englishman looked for a virgin corner of his hankie with which to clean his glasses.

We passed the Ministry of Culture, and the museum: the speechless poets—blind painters—a tingling in the sculptor's amputated hands . . .

"AND NOW we're going to lose this person," the Britisher said, "pretty much as they do in a film. Do I gather as much?"

"It isn't stupid," I insisted. "It's a workable idea."

We both got out of the cab at one of the entrances to the Mercado Central. "Anyway I'm out of shampoo."

In this post-cataclysmic vastness, where once there'd been some kind of downtown, the Mercado lay like a small island. "If he leaves his car here, and we lose him on the other side, he'll have a hard time getting transportation."

"Right, I see it now," the Brit said. "Certainly give it a try if you like."

"I don't speak Spanish very well," I told the cabbie. "If you don't understand, please tell me that you don't understand."

"I understand," he said. "We'll meet on the other side of the Mercado."

"And I'll give you the second part of this." I tore a hundred-cordoba note in two and gave him half.

He looked at his half, and then at me, in utter horror. "I understand," he said.

We left him. "Do you think he'll be there?"

"Oh, there must be cabs on the other side," I said. "I just don't remember for sure."

"Are you certain you can walk all right?"

"You insist I'm plastered. I'm doing fine. I have the use of my legs."

"Very good."

The Englishman kept looking back, embarrassed and self-conscious and pretending otherwise. "Are we still . . ."

"We're still being monitored."

The OIJ man was walking about twenty feet behind. He wasn't looking at merchandise. He was looking at us.

"It occurs to me—what do you suppose he'll—what action," the Brit finally managed to say, "is he going to take when he sees we're trying to lose him?"

"Oh I guess he'll shoot you in the back once or twice."

He was taken with a shudder.

"Just kidding," I assured him.

"Indeed."

"I need some shampoo."

"Shampoo. Oh, well, as long as we're here then," he said, "surrounded by shampoo."

We were a long time travelling down the weird thoroughfares at the Mercado, a maze of shops on the order of a Stateside shopping mall, but laid out more haphazardly and quite a bit more various in its pretensions, the decor of sad fifties bowling alleys and modest living rooms, country sheds, Alabama shoeshine parlors, phone booths, and so on pressed out in a series of shops devoted to the sale of any item, absolutely any item, but mostly, as elsewhere, the most useless items: U.S. junk, cheap digital watches, imitation designer jeans, tee-shirts stamped with the spectral-sexual symbols of Heavy Metal rock groups, cuddly posters and records and jogging shoes, something like home but slightly, horribly askew because so much of it was secondhand, dented, bent, stained, or just inexplicable . . . We passed a closed government office whose interior was dominated by an old round-shouldered Coke machine . . .

"I got to have some rum," I said.

"Must be some of that in the vicinity too, I should think."

Next to a store that sold both used furniture and costume jewelry we found a store that sold both rum and shampoo.

The OIJ man waited outside like an angry friend. Leaving the shop, we were walking right toward him.

"It does get you standing up straight, doesn't it?"

"Adrenaline. It's a beautiful hit," I said.

I meant to say hello as we passed, but nervousness pinched shut my throat. And there was an intimacy in being so near to him that depressed me . . .

"I should get my hair washed by a real professional," I was suddenly moved to say.

But the only hairdresser's we passed was empty and dark. Most of the stores were closed. The others were closing.

Our man stayed with us all the way, neither obtrusive nor hidden. I couldn't help thinking of a spirit wandering in the Bardo between its death and the next birth, trailing behind its future parents, as we came out the Mercado's other side and found the roadway in the big absence cleared by the seventies' earthquake.

"I see there are two cabs."

"Take ours," I said, "I'll race you."

"Ours is the slower one, I'm sure of it."

"Just to the other side of the field," I said, "right there where the road curves." The OIJ man, who'd caught on, was bearing down fast. "Go! Go!"

The whole idea nearly fell through because the OIJ spoke quickly and volubly, confusing my driver with frightening promises, as he closed the distance between us. "Fuck him! Fuck him!" I told the cabbie tearfully.

The car we'd come in was already away, carrying the Englishman.

"Fuck him!" the cabbie cried, much amused. "Let's rock!" He squealed the tires leaving.

"You just made a thousand cordobas."

We pulled abreast of the other cab, and the drivers played games while I signalled to the other and talked to mine, until I'd convinced them both, with some difficulty, that we should stop after only a few hundred yards.

I paid off my driver extravagantly and fell, with a creaking of brittle upholstery, into the seat next to the Britisher. "Brilliant! Brilliant!" he said as our cab crept away.

The field floated in the dusk.

"Nothing matters, does it?" he said as he watched me sip from the bottle.

"Not for you anymore," I said, "and it never did for me."

"I have to disagree on both counts," he said.

"Look at him out there. He really would shoot you, I bet."

The Costa Rican was standing across the field watching us.

"Right." He took my hand and laughed. "I can feel it."

IN FRONT of my place, as I was paying off the cab, the Englishman asked me, "Where did you get so much money?" It really wasn't his kind of question. He was so tense he didn't know what he was saying.

"In Costa Rica." It had been foregone that he'd come back to the Whatsis Motel with me. "Watch out for the dog-do," I warned him, "watch out for the kiddy-plop." Back at the Inter-Continental, the representatives of his fate would be hanging around.

"I'm sure it's all been driven down into the mud. My God, what a rain. What muck. Oh, here's a clear puddle." Under the awning there was a slab of concrete in which a basin had been eroded. He soaked the bottoms of his shoes and I washed my feet in the puddle there. "You were marvelous," he said. "You're a treasure. You, the rain, the escape—"

Such gush embarrassed me. "By Jove," I told him, "I thought you English were supposed to be steely and reserved."

Now he was the one embarrassed. "No, those are the chaps with pith helmets and years of training." As we went in he said again, "My God, what a rain."

The Señora greeted us, coming from the back, rubbing the sleep from her face, a tiny woman, somewhat hump-backed, her hair tied up in a scarf . . . I hadn't yet determined if she was actually this outfit's owner or just an impassioned hireling.

"Any calls?" I said in English.

"Good evening," she said in Spanish.

She turned on the hi-fi and set about doing her books at

the desk. Actually, I knew, she meant to serve as chaperone should the situation require one—in her friendly presence and drunk out of my mind I could adhere to the couch with my state-of-shock boyfriend and listen to music, hey.

She was just as happy that we went on through the lobby and into my room.

"NOTHING fancy," I tell him.

"The bulbs are very dim . . ."

"Bulb. There's only one bulb."

I relieve my purse of its bulge in the bathroom and discover that the administration of this motel, meaning some sneaky relation of the Señora's, has also been looting the Inter-Continental: instead of the usual stack of carefully torn squares of newsprint, a folded yard of bluish toilet paper rests on the tank of the commode. It's 1984, the real 1984, the revolution's over and things are looking up.

He's standing by the window but you can't see a thing out there through the screen with the light behind you, what does he think he's looking at?

"I see you have a back door," he says.

"These rooms were originally hired by the hour. This used to be a triste-motel. You come in the back door, you pay through this window." I show him the small window, like a ticket-seller's, next to the door that opens onto the hall. "You pay as you go, from hour to hour. Nobody gets your name, nobody sees your face."

"Oh, for a life like that."

The rain starts again. But not too hard. He looks up through the ceiling toward the weather.

"No more," he says. "This is too much." His blue jacket hits the floor.

He lies down on the bed.

I fall on the bed next to him, and inside me it all comes loose. I put one foot on the floor to keep the room from spinning . . .

The Señora goes by outside in the hallway, humming a love song along with Radio Tempo. I've never brought a man here before now, but the Señora understands, time is a river ever moving, chastity's a joke this year, it's 1984, there's a war on, and the radios are crying, just as they're probably crying in New York, "You take my self, you take my self-control."

Beside me he falls asleep, still wearing one of his shoes.

H O W M A N Y mornings am I going to wake and find him there, this one, that one, or another one, one who last night seemed so sad and forgivable, last night in a moment when I myself was framed with a blessed light, borne down on soft wings, how many mornings, having forgotten his name, am I going to wake up and find him there in my bed like a slab of meat?

I didn't have to open my eyes. I only had to listen for his breathing to know that the troubled Englishman was still with me.

At some point he'd got up and undressed himself. He lay uncovered, turned away from me, a big thing with a hidden face—for all I knew, he'd left in the night and been replaced by some other incompetent—wearing boxer undershorts of the kind any fool might have prophesied.

By this time, morning at the Whatsis had been happening for hours, and the moans and rattles from the other parts of the building had settled into the day's monotony. "I smell coffee in Dogpatch," I said.

He was too unconscious to be roused. He'd be sorry if he slept very late—this wasn't the air-conditioned Inter-Continental. In bed past ten-thirty, he'd be broiled alive. Already perspiration dripped out of his hair and down his neck as he slept.

What point was there trying to sleep? I'd only at some point wake up again. I had to go out anyway, I had errands, I had to go out. I had to go out of the country, it suddenly occurred to me as it seemed to do quite often, or go out of my mind.

By now it was light enough to see that there weren't any bugs around the drain: I took a brief shower—only cold water here—and washed my hair with Prell, newly bought but so old the label's print had faded white. I put on clean clothes.

Pilar, or whatever her name was—the washer-woman and Five-Star General of Maids—was resting on the couch.

"Coffee?" I asked her. "With milk?"

"Black coffee," she corrected me, and went to get it.

I STAYED at La Whatsis cheaply, that is, at the recommended official rate as opposed to the actual, usual one, thanks to an impotent (our little secret) Vice-minister at Interturismo.

This man at Interturismo had told me many times he had a contact, a cousin, an uncle, who knows what, but someone willing, anyway, to turn cordobas into dollars.

I'd never tried him out, because I'd never been so desperate as to want to believe this obvious lie, never so greedy as to traffic with Contras right here in the capital of their extermination, never wanted to owe favors to the future dead —until now. And what for? Did I think I'd be "rolled up" in some kind of currency investigation? Over the course of weeks I'd gone back to Interpren time after time after time, just to get a couple of documents . . . If it took years to fill the blanks in a press card, think what centuries must drip past before the machinery of prosecution for some picayune commercial misdemeanor started up. Certainly it wasn't a consideration to run me out of here any faster than anything else.

Hung over and fueled by a general irritation, I was at last moving, that's all . . .

Oh once again trying to make clear what can't be understood or forgiven . . .

I CALLED the Vice-minister from one of the shell-shaped pay phones on the corner near the motel where the taxis waited empty on the dirt shoulder and the houses were silent. He was an old man, one of the few grown-ups still functioning in an official capacity, I liked him, he treated me like an errant daughter, et cetera, and this morning he seemed to convey assurances from a far planet as his voice drifted, competing with a giant hum, down the wires. I gathered he was glad to hear from me.

"Please speak very loudly and slowly," I said.

"Yes, okay."

I said, "Do you remember that you said you had a friend?"

"Yes, I remember," he said.

"A friend to help me with my cordobas."

"Yes. I remember our conversation."

"I'd like to contact him."

"Yes," he said.

"Can you tell me how to contact him?"

"Yes, I can."

"Can you tell me now, on the telephone?"

"No, I can't."

"When can you give me the information?"

"Come to my office," he said.

"Soon?"

"Before noon."

"I'll come right now."

"Certainly, but don't hurry . . ."

I'd never been able, actually I'd never tried, to find out what the taxis thought they were doing parked here, driverless, on this dirt shoulder, and it never failed to rankle me that I had to walk a block and a half to the nearest substantial intersection and stand, still within sight of them and usually for quite a while, until I got a live one and was carried off— in this case across the city to the corner where the Interturismo offices were.

From before this bureau's gates I could see one of the town's better restaurants, and a corner of the parking lot of the patio café I called Los Paraquitos, and beyond that the Inter-Continental Hotel looming like a mountain, tall enough to have afforded the journalists a view of Nicaragua's government changing hands, one hand dropping bombs on the other, five years earlier.

My Vice-minister friend was busy and sent me over to the restaurant. There was nothing to do there. I looked at *La Barricada*. It was a day of wreckage in the papers: Something had crashed just after take-off from Timbuktu . . . And on Monday a C-47 piloted out of Honduras had been shot down in the north.

The waiter brought me a menu.

"Do you have a Coke?"

"No Coke."

I got some livid violet fruit juice in which floated a shard of ice.

I liked the Vice-minister not only because he liked me, but because he found me beautiful.

I've never been beautiful. Currently I was too thin, but whenever I gain weight it goes on in uncoordinated bulges.

My face is appealing although I have bad teeth . . . I'm not beautiful but I keep my back straight and my hands still.

"I'm leaving Managua," I told the Vice-minister as soon as he got there.

He beheld me with weariness and amusement. "When?"

"Very soon. In a few days, I think."

"Going back to the United States?"

"I want to go to San José. Maybe after that, I'll visit Playas del Coco."

"It's not the season for Playas. If you want to go back to Costa Rica, Limón would be more interesting."

"Too crowded there," I said in English. "Crowded?"

"No crowded. But a person can be losted there."

"I like Playas. It's quiet."

"Then go to Playas," he said, getting back to Spanish. "And I suppose you need some Costa Rican money?"

"I need U.S. in order to buy a plane ticket."

"Very bad."

"Can't your friend get U.S.?"

"Maybe. But I don't think so."

Bright promises turning vague . . . Such was the plot of every transaction, human or financial, in this bed of dung!

"Are you still living at the motel whose management I spoke to?"

"Yes."

"It's okay for you there, I believe?"

"Yes. I'm used to it."

"Maybe you should stay there a little longer."

"Can you buy a ticket for me with cordobas? A ticket to San José?"

He smiled. "I don't believe I'll be permitted to buy a plane ticket to Costa Rica."

I SEEMED to be getting into the very Latin habit of
going over and going over my options without committing
myself to, or even coming up with, an actual plan . . .

In the taxi to Plaza España where this money marketeer
kept his offices, I tried to lock my attention onto the problems
ahead of me and mislaid all sense of the goal. The fumes and
smells and roaring temperature of Managua's roadways sav-
aged all mental effort, in my brain was only a kind of tape-
hiss. As I got out of the cab before the white, two-tiered
Plaza, the kind of moneyed-Texas architecture Nicaragua had
once esteemed, I found I'd lost my mind and could only wonder, What errand has driven me here? Young boys who would
soon be killers approached me, demanding money. "Right."
It was money I'd come for. "Thank you," I said, making
headway through them toward the offices, "fuck you," I added,
"you're wasting your time."

And then I wasted a good deal of my own time trying to
find the place, a travel agency, ironically.

But of course much more time would be wasted before
anything was accomplished—that is the style. Whatever happened, nothing would happen today, I'd have to go back
again—you have to appear at least twice, anywhere, in order
to prove your existence.

I found him at the appointed place, behind the desk of his
travel agency, which, by the look of it, hadn't been open for
business in quite a while.

Like his friend the Vice-minister, who'd begged off ac-
companying me here because it was risky for a person in his
position, this one was an older man.

The venetian blinds were drawn. The fixture for the overhead fluorescent was empty. And a study-lamp bending low

over his desk gave the only light. "Good day. Good day," he said. He only needed sunglasses on his face to make it all just too nauseatingly sinister to bear.

I said, "Your office is closed permanently?"

"Why? You wish to go somewhere today?" This was said by another man who now leaned into the light, wearing sunglasses. A boy, really, with smooth skin and the frailest beginnings of a moustache.

The older man smiled and offered me a seat. "We can probably arrange travel for you. But I don't think you want it."

I offered them cigarets, and they assured me that the Vice-minister had been in touch.

We all three smoked, fouling the room, and I declined their offer of coffee.

"It's strange that you have an office, but no commerce."

"No, it's not strange . . ." He made a speech that I couldn't keep up with, but I understood he saw no point in running a travel agency when hardly anyone could be expected to travel anywhere.

I said, "This is a time of poverty. The shortages, no replacements . . ." Most of my Spanish came off the wall-posters and out of the pages of *La Barricada* . . . "I have a problem about money, too."

"It's no problem," he said. "For someone who knows the methods, it's not a problem, the lack of replacements . . ." I lost him, and then regained the meaning a couple of sentences later . . . "I live at a height above those things."

He closed his eyes on all of it. "Another floor," he said in English, "another room."

"Then you can help me, I believe."

"Are you fond of eggs? I have chickens at my house."

"Oh, yes."

"I can get milk at my comrade's house. And the man who

gives gas coupons right here in the Plaza España is my cousin.
I can buy extra coupons from him at a good price."

"I have no car. I don't need coupons."

"I'm not trying to sell you coupons. I'm saying something.
I live at a height above this war, this shit. My children aren't
going to fight for the Sandinistas."

"Good. War is bad."

"Sandinistas are bad."

"Can you get drugs?"

"What do you want."

I shrugged. "Cocaine?"

"You're crazy. Go to Panama."

"I don't really want cocaine."

"Then why do you ask? Why do you drink when you're
not thirsty?"

I shrugged again. I felt stupid. It had only been a notion.

"Watch out for the woman who drinks when she's not
thirsty."

"Yes," I said, "I'll watch out."

"No. It's a saying of the Miskitos. It tells me to watch
out, not you."

"All right then goddamn it," I burst out in English, "keep
your fucking eye on me then, okay?"

He paused, shocked. "I know very little English," he said,
"but I know 'goddamn' and I know 'fuck.' 'Fuck' is the prop-
erty of the whole world."

"I need to exchange cordobas for dollars," I said.

"Everybody wants that. Even the members of the Junta
would like dollars."

"Can you do that for me?"

"I have a problem too," he now revealed.

"Yes. How can I help?"

"You are a journalist."

"Yes."

"You understand about this country. The Sandinistas are bad. If they decide I'm a Contra, then it doesn't matter, they'll arrest me. If they can't arrest me, they'll arrest my family. Maybe I'm a Contra. Maybe I'm not Contra."

"I understand," I lied, completely sorry that I'd come here.

"My mother hasn't done anything," he said. "My sister hasn't done anything. But they're both in prison."

"Ah."

"You're a journalist, a North American—if you ask about her, my sister, my mother—it will be a big help. Show them you know the names of my mother and sister."

He gave me a piece of paper bearing their names.

"If I can," I said.

"You can. Go to the Office of Defense. It's only one street away from Interturismo, do you know it? Ask them what's become of these two people. They'll believe these names are known in the United States. Things will go better for my mother and sister, do you see?"

"I see."

"And then we can help you. We need to make arrangements. Tell us what you'd like, and we'll arrange it for tomorrow."

"What rate of exchange do you offer?" I felt miserable, sick, and confused.

"The rate of exchange must be decided tomorrow."

"And you'll have dollars tomorrow?"

"I don't think so. But my companion will help you."

The other looked too young to help anybody, even himself.

"Why do you want cocaine?" he said.

"It was a mistake to talk about cocaine," I said. "I'm nervous. My Spanish is very poor . . ."

"No one here will give you cocaine."

"I understand. I made a mistake."

"We barter currency."

"I understand. I'm sorry. What time will I come back tomorrow?"

"What time would you like to come back tomorrow," he said.

"I can come about nine o'clock."

"In the morning?"

"If that's not too early."

"It's fine. In the meantime, permit me to take your passport. I'll make a photocopy in just a few minutes. I want to verify you."

"I don't want you to verify me."

"Then I have no money for you. No U.S. I have Swiss."

"Swiss?"

"It can be exchanged fast, not here, but in San José, in Honduras, U.S."

"What about Costa Rican?"

"Nothing today."

"I need U.S. or Costa Rican."

In English he said, "Yew air estewpid."

"What."

"You tell me where you go. I go Costa Rica, I go U.S." He went on in Spanish, "Nothing is verified about me but you're talking. This is exactly what an American woman is. Our women have learned a new way. It's a war."

"If I go to get a photocopy, will you wait?"

"We'll be here until three o'clock," the older man said.

It wasn't yet two. "I need dollars only. U.S. Only U.S.," I said. "I'll bring a photocopy of my passport."

"Good," he said.

The other said, "She doesn't honor us with her faith. She doesn't trust her friends."

"It's true," I said.

"It's good," the first said, as he rose to show me out the door.

It was hotter outside, but I noticed I wasn't perspiring as much, not half as much.

Your passport. In every encounter they wanted my face, and they wanted my name . . .

I knew of a copying service not too far off—I'd often passed the sign—the place was nothing more than a shack squatting on a mound directly across the street from the Cultural Center. I went there right away and poked my head through the doorway.

Inside, a solemn man in a white shirt, wearing a necktie, tinkered with his machine. There was hardly any light to see by. "It's not ready," he said. "One moment." There was a lamp on a tripod, a chair for photographees, a tiny curtained closet where I gathered he developed his photos. The floor was earth. He'd quickly removed the outer case of his photo-copier and now he was gently violating the mystery of its robot ganglia with a penknife.

I moved to the doorway and smoked a cigaret in the bar-rage of traffic noise. The road narrowed here, and the suicide-macho rattleheaps contended for the only lane, while the pods of the giant frangipanis wept down onto their hoods. In a few minutes the man said, "It's ready."

I gave him my passport to copy, but the machine still didn't work. "There's nothing I can do," he said with the terrible sadness of a heart surgeon.

It was only two-thirty when I was already back at the defunct travel office, knocking repeatedly on the door and rattling the knob and getting no answer at all from those bastards.

I saw it plainly, I'd go back time and again to see people I couldn't make myself clear to . . . I'd spend forever listening to irrelevancies . . . The whole matter would get impossibly snarled . . . In the end I would take whatever I got, and gladly . . .

By the power of my desperation I forced a pay phone to function and called that worthless homo, the Vice-minister.

"Come in and talk to me," he said. He was speaking English.

I hesitated.

"You must. It's safe."

"Why are you talking English?"

"Because I want to talk to you only."

"What do you mean," I said, "*It's safe?*"

"Will you come here—today," he said. "I can't find the word. Now. Right now you come."

"Is it about the money? Your friends? I'm looking for your friends."

"No, it's another business, something that isn't for me—they don't tell to me."

"*Who* doesn't tell you?"

"Please come now."

Nothing ever happened over these phones. "Okay. I'll get a cab."

He hung up.

And it was exactly then, I believe, that I made my mistake, the gesture up out of the flames that brought me to the attention of the torturer.

Because I happened to be at a functioning phone, clutching some change in my hand, I dropped in two cordobas and dialed the Inter-Continental. I thought I'd call Mr. Watts Oil and arrange a meeting; I'd fill him in on whatever the Vice-minister was about to tell me—after all, this new issue of "safety" probably arose from the Englishman's activities as a blabbermouth, it seemed to me.

I'd keep the Englishman abreast, I'd do the Englishman a favor. In this place, a favor!

I didn't know why I should want to help him even a little.

When I called the Inter-Continental, he wasn't there. I told them I'd leave a message.

"He has check out."

Oh. Ah.

"Smart man," I said. "Do you mean he's taken his luggage and everything?"

"Yes."

So the Englishman wasn't there. I did him no favor.

But I swear to you that I've tracked it down to that, each bit of it, going backward, from the moment much later in the holy rain when I finally identified every one of us—you, me, him, the Devil, God . . .

From that moment many lifetimes later in the jungle cathedral, I've traced it back step by step to that thwarted, fated try at calling the sucker from Watts Oil: that attempt to help one of these miserable victims. It started there.

NOT TWENTY minutes later I stood at the doors of the Interturismo offices while the Vice-minister, heading me off before I could announce myself to his secretary, warned me, "You down espik espunish, you down espik espunish . . ." He introduced me to his secretary himself: "This is Miss America. She doesn't speak Spanish."

His secretary, a beautiful young lady in a red pantsuit to whom I'd spoken a good deal of Spanish only yesterday, smiled at me.

The Vice-minister also smiled at me. "It's no good at all," he said in English. "A very bad situation." This last word pronounced, not inappropriately, "stewation."

He took me into the hallway, and then the staircase. "I think you must begin to move. Go right now. Go to any place. Managua is no good at all."

"No good at all? That's not exactly *news*."

"The people come from the Department of Defense to talk about you."

"They will come? Or they already came."

"Yes, it's not clear, excuse me, they already came a little time ago. This is no good. They were very bad to me, muy brusco. They wish to talk about you."

"What did they ask you?"

"They want me to help them find you, and we will take away your passport."

"My *passport*! Did you tell them where I live?"

"No. But they can find out. It will be fast."

"What did I *do*?"

"Something very bad. Go away of Managua, right now, today."

"This is crazy. Can't you come outside and tell me in Spanish?"

"No. We're finish talking right now. Goodbye. I tell you it's very bad, it's enough. Please, for you it's enough now."

"Your secretary *knows* I speak Spanish. I was in here *yester*day."

"Goodbye, Señorita."

Only last week I'd held his head to my breast, kissed the spots on his scalp showing through the thin hair . . . All his life he'd wanted so willing a woman, but these days he was useless . . . Only last week! we'd been naked together and his fat thighs had hung down and he'd cried . . . "Please," I said. "Please."

He began breathing rapidly in a way that meant he was going to be stubborn. "Señorita," he said reverently and sadly, and shrugged. "No more is possible."

Okay—no more was possible. "I appreciate what you've been able to do," I forced myself to say.

"You are nice to be courteous," he said. "And also, goodbye."

W H E N I got back to La Whatsis I entered the lobby, and it was just as if nothing had ever happened to me and nothing ever would. In the lobby the Señora relaxed and fanned herself slowly with a newspaper, while Radio Tempo sang to her and one more meaningless day died into history. Of course she did; it was crazy to do anything else.

The Englishman was in my room, sitting on the bed. I thought I might be able to save myself if I could just get rid of this man.

"The Señora let you in?" I asked.

"Haven't I been hiding here all day?"

"What are you planning to do?" I said to him.

"I have no idea *what* to plan, except that I'd better get to London. And I don't want to talk to any more Costa Ricans. I thought I'd better ask you about how to proceed."

"I can't suggest a thing. You're all screwed up over at the Inter-Continental, is all I know—anyway, they told me you'd packed up and left."

"Well, certainly. I left last night."

"They told me you checked out."

"Checked *out* did you say?"

"I could've gotten it wrong. It was over the phone. And also, did you know the Department of Defense is after you?" It seemed best not to include myself in this news.

He made a vague limp-wristed gesture. He wasn't taking this in at quite the rate of presentation.

"You never said anything about those guys, the Defense people."

"Well, they're all the same to me. I hadn't really thought anybody was *after* me. This OIJ fellow wanted to keep tabs, that was my impression."

"Listen," I said, "it's probably not as serious as we've been thinking."

"I'm absolutely at a loss," he said. "Absolutely. Completely. I don't know what to do now."

"Why don't you go back to the Inter-Continental and get this taken care of? Confront them? Staying here won't help."

"I don't think I should confront *any*body. I don't want to

be detained in this country. I've got to get back to London right away."

"Well you can't stay here, honey. I'm sorry, but that's the condensed version. If I let you stay I'll end up wishing I'd never met you."

"Please help me," he begged, goddamn him, "somebody's got to check the hotel for me. And somehow I've got to change my airline reservation without being detained. If you'd please give me some assistance, if you'd check for me at the hotel in person . . . Wait, that's it, that's just the thing—you go to my hotel, ask for me in person . . ."

He seemed to be *fixating* on this idea of asking for him at the hotel. Did he expect I'd find him in? "Look," I told him, "I promise I'll try to change your airline reservation, and straighten out your life, and what else, help you get dollars somehow—I'm seeing these two guys tomorrow, in fact. I'll ask about what they can do with an American Express card, or whatever you carry."

"I've got traveller's checks."

"On you?"

"On me?"

"I mean do you have them with you?"

"No," he said, "they're at the hotel."

"There's nothing at the hotel, they say. The lady said your luggage was gone."

"Oh, my God," he said. "It didn't register when you first mentioned it."

"Well, is it registering now?"

Who was this person? Had he been assigned by his head office to lose himself in the labyrinth of my arrangements, and land at my door starving?

"All right. I'm tired and I've got to rest," I told him. "Fend for yourself."

I lay down on the bed. Was there any air at all in this

horrible room? It was the worst time of day to be indoors—
or outdoors, if it came to that; it was the worst time of day.
Even before he was done bothering me with his next question, I was asleep . . .

And woke I didn't know how much later . . .

He was sitting on the floor, resting his shoulders against
the bed and paging through *La Biblia*, one of my very few
books. "They say all the answers are in there, if you can de-
cipher that tiny print." I felt lazy and serene.

"All unintelligible to you, is it?" he said.

"No. It's just that the print's too small and too blurry."

"Try these." He handed me his glasses over his shoulder,
and I put them on.

Everything became elongated, and somehow both two-
and three-dimensional. Somewhat like the view through pay-
binoculars—but how much sharper, how extra-crisp! I looked
over his shoulder at the print. "God, these work!"

"You must need glasses, I'd imagine."

"I can read all right,"

"Maybe you're nearsighted."

"No, I see fine if I hold the book up close."

"Well, that's what it means to be nearsighted."

I put the book away.

"Is your Spanish good?" he asked.

"I can read newspapers. The Bible's a little beyond me."

"Then why do you keep it right here by the bed?"

"To read. I do read it, it's all that's left—it's the only
thing that hasn't been torn up for toilet paper. I just don't
read it very well, is all."

"The painted lady with the Bible in a foreign tongue, the
undecipherable Bible. Something poetic in that, hey?"

"I've got two English books, too. American. Poems, as a
matter of fact."

As soon as I got up to rifle my suitcase for the rest of my

library, I felt the sweat travelling my spine. Wouldn't the day's rain ever fall? "I know a poem that's written just for fugitives like you on a hot day like this." I handed him the book open to the place.

"Oh do you," he said.

I'd forgotten what the poem was about but I knew it ended by saying, "It is Sunday."

It is Sunday forever and begins to snow.
I am going into the snow
as I have wanted to do for years.

"It fits, huh?"

He tensed, as if memorizing these lines, or maybe himself. "Yes. You might say that."

"James L. Whatever. A true denizen of Hell."

"Lives in Hell, does he then?" I could see all this talk was eating at his moorings. He looked at the cover. "White. James L. White."

"A former inhabitant, actually. Poets who live in Hell go to Heaven when they die."

"An interesting mythology begins to emerge . . ."

He lay down beside me on the bed.

In a minute or two his eyes fell closed and consciousness began bubbling up out through the lids . . . If you want to sleep as certainly as if you'd overdosed, it's simple, lay yourself down in a soft place under one of these baking roofs. Just as you think you'll expire of the sweat, you lose touch with all the world's unkindness . . . In a while, who knows how long, we opened our eyes and found each other. It was too hot to make love, but we were awake now and there was nothing else to do . . . He didn't understand. He was looking at me warily. "We'll bring the price down," I said. He said: "I wouldn't want you to cheapen yourself," and I said, "Well, you know what they say—there's no such thing as a hundred-dollar whore; there are only twenty-dollar whores and hundred-dollar customers." "No," he said, "I hadn't heard that one." We were kissing all through this. We were dying of thirst, we were drinking each other. I was so aroused I felt my controls giving way. I put him inside of me.

Later, in the middle of it, because it felt momentarily true, I told him, "You're the best I ever had . . ."

Then we just lay beside each other. It would take us decades to cool off. His pale skin was blotched red, as if making love, for him, was unhealthy and dangerous. "And was there something of a discount then," he said. It was obvious he felt some childish, also in my opinion boorish, excitement over having dredged for himself one small free lunch in all this jungle. And of course he was looking better and better to me: the blood had raged into my eyes, I couldn't see straight. I'd liked him from the first minute, it seemed, but until just now I hadn't liked his looks . . .

He said, "What did you do Stateside, do you mind my asking."

"Oh well, you know. A little of this and a little of that."

"And mostly a little of this, I suppose."

"No! Well, one semester I picked up some extra money, in college. Money," I said, "with which to visit the museums."

"You're beautiful. Beautiful."

I laughed, covering my bad teeth.

We fell asleep again.

I WOKE up. I was alone. I pulled on my skirt and blouse and stuck my head out the door.

The Englishman was sitting at the desk in the lobby, and he was in a state. "I've been trying to phone the airline for half an hour. It's maddening—the bloody phone's an instrument of torture, nothing more. It goes on ringing, it's un-believable—is anybody in today at all?"

"The phone's a joke. So why aren't you laughing? Every-body knows the phone's a joke."

"I'll have to go right down to British Airways and see them in person."

"And tomorrow you're going to have to go right back again," I warned him. "You have to go everywhere twice before anything happens."

He sat back in the Señora's swivel chair and looked at the lobby. The sun was falling through the door, and a yellow fog of dust moved in the light. The Señora was sitting on the divan next to the hi-fi with her feet flat on the floor and her knees apart and her eyes closed, fanning herself with her news-paper in her sleep. "The airlines," the Brit said, "are com-puterized."

"Kind of like the telephones," I suggested.

"I *did* get through to the desk at the hotel. They're clear enough that I'm no longer registered there."

"And?"

"And beyond that we don't seem to communicate."

I took the phone from him and dialed the Inter-Continental.

"I certainly haven't checked out of there myself—are you ringing them, I hope."

I got a desk clerk on the line and she told me the same thing again. "She says you've checked out."

"Let me talk to her."

"Were you there when he left?" I asked the clerk.

"I don't remember," she said.

"Please, may I . . . ?"

I gave him the receiver.

"I haven't checked out of anywhere," he said. "Excuse me —I am *he*, you see. I beg your pardon? Un momento— Now," he told me, covering the receiver with his hand, "she's speaking in Spanish and I can't understand."

"They always do that. It means she doesn't want to talk to you."

He handed me back the phone and I said, "Were you at the desk when he checked out of the hotel?"

"The Watts Oil travel representative checked out for him and removed his baggage."

"Somebody took your luggage," I told him. And I told the clerk, "Very bad. He's with me now. He wanted to stay."

"He must contact his companions at Watts Oil right away."

"There's been a mistake. Can you help us?" I asked her.

"The best way to start is by talking to his companions at Watts Oil," she repeated.

"Now we get a thousand helpful suggestions and no fucking help whatsoever," I let him know.

"For heaven's sake, get the *manager* on the line," he said.

"I want to talk to the manager," I said.

"He isn't here right now."

"At what time will he come back?"

"I'm not sure. Perhaps after supper. Perhaps eight o'clock."

"Thanks." I hung up. "You'll have to go in person," I said. "Don't bother with the phones down here. Same with the British Airways—go in person."

The Motel Whatsis's driveway was only a rut worn in the grass out front and curving out of sight beside the building. The whole time I'd been dialing and talking, I now realized, I'd been looking right at the front fender of a vehicle parked just around the building's corner—wearyingly identical to the front fender of a Daihatsu jeep.

"Look at that," I told the Englishman. "Wait a minute."

Stepping out under the awning and creeping out past its shadow, I ascertained that the jeep had Costa Rican license plates; at which point I meant to back off, but the Costa Rican had already seen me, and so I came all the way round the building's edge.

"Excuse me," the Costa Rican said in English. He struck an attitude, one foot up on the rear bumper, polishing his sunglasses with a white handkerchief. His face was a cipher.

For some reason I laughed out loud. I suppose I was confused.

"Something funny?"

"No. Nothing."

"Oh no? But still you're laughing. What is your name, please?"

"Oh," I said, "I have a bad head for names."

"Please, hey, wait a minute," he said. "I was in the U.S. for four years. I got married to my wife there. One of my girls she is going to school right now in Ann Arbor. So don't fuck with me. That's my statement."

He put his sunglasses on and folded his handkerchief and put it in his pocket.

"Well," I said after a long, dull minute—because I was frightened, and felt as if I needed his permission—"I'm going back inside now."

"*Ho*-kay, excuse me, no." He closed his eyes and shook his head. He opened his eyes. "I told you already once, don't fuck with me, or I'm gonna fuck with you. You better let me take your passport, because I'm gonna make a photocopy."

"I can't give you my passport."

He held out his hand.

"I can't give you my passport."

"I know that your England friend is inside," he said. "Did you think you were going to play a fucking game?"

"I can't really talk to you."

"What do you believe? Do you believe this is nothing? Do you believe you take this guy through the Mercado, fuck him, it's fun, and then it's finished? Did you fuck him?" He grabbed my wrist.

"Let go."

"I'm listening right outside the window, bitch. Do you know who's playing in your game? A lot of people."

I could see he was in pain. "A lot of people?" I said. I was so frightened of him I couldn't swallow.

"You're not gonna fuck him and then you just say, like that, it's finish. You're gonna have a lot of explanation to take care of. Goddamn it!" He shook his head. "Another fucking cunt playing games."

"Okay," I said, breaking free of his hold on my arm. "Señora! Call the cops! Señora!" I ran through the door into the lobby. It was empty. The lock was on the phone.

"The *cops!*" I heard him say with hard, false laughter, but he made no move to follow me through the door.

As soon as I saw the Englishman in my room, my heart fell. Just for those few seconds I'd assumed he'd run somewhere far away and I was done with him.

Well, but I wasn't done with him. Somewhat stupidly I asked him, "Did you see who was out there?"

"Yes, I did. That's why I've come in here."

For the next few minutes we each behaved as if the other weren't around. Our panic eliminated all belief in what was happening. I went into the bathroom and stood before the commode, baffled and blank, until I decided I must be looking for a cigaret.

He, meanwhile, sat on the bed looking between his knees at the floor with his glasses slipped down to the end of his nose.

Out in the lobby Radio Tempo was playing one I hadn't heard—a black song, hard-rock disco, you might call it: *Oh, baby, kick my butt—I'd love to kick your butt . . .*

I never found out what Radio Tempo thought it was or

who in the world ran it. Its programming was unearthly. The gringo rhythms and Top 40 phrases hanging in the sodden air—*I wanna; bay-hubee; shake, shake, shake; c'mown now*—evidenced that we were using up our tiny lives, going around in these ridiculous circles, along the outflung fingers of an empire.

"Have you got a cigaret for me?" I asked him.

"Oh. Sure," he said.

I opened the door to see if it was the Señora who'd turned up the radio, or just the housekeeper.

But it was the Costa Rican, sitting in a chair. He had his feet up on the hi-fi, and his eyes were closed.

I shut the door softly. "This man scares me."

"He's still out there, then."

"That's him. What is he trying to do?"

"He's—I don't know."

"All right, all right," I said, "but who is he working with up here? I mean what does he think he's doing up *here*?"

"He's nobody here really. He's completely out of his area. I don't know if he's on a private mission, or if he's in touch with—whoever. But I wish he would go away, I can tell you that."

"Maybe you should talk to him. I think you should talk to him. You're not going to London till you get all this straightened out. You've got to face some people. *You're* supposed to face them, but it's *my* window they're peeking into. Oh, please. You're a businessman. Don't you have contacts?"

"My contacts are no good. Do you have contacts?"

"A Vice-minister at Interturismo, and a Sub-tenente at Interpren. The vice-ministers and the sub-tenentes, that's who I know. The slobs and losers. And they both just got done cutting me loose."

"Too bad. You struck me as somewhat the Mata Hari."

"This is a real revolution—the rot doesn't climb any higher than the underlings. I never even get introduced to the other ones, the ones without a prefix on their rank."

"Well then, won't you get in touch with *some*body? This man at Interturismo, for instance, can he help me get back to the UK?"

"He's the one who turned us in, it had to be him. The worthless coward!"

"Maybe he saw no other way."

"There *is* no other way. That's how it works down here."

"In any case, he can't help. What about your magazine?"

I had to laugh. "*Roundup Magazine*? They talk to me on the phone, but they don't do anything else. They're no help. Look," I said, "I can't help you."

"What sort of articles do you write for them?"

"I don't write any articles for them," I confessed. "I just talk to them on the phone. Once they sent me money."

"Just let me stay. I'll be out of your life tomorrow—I can't *think*." The idea seemed to startle him. "My mind honestly will not function. It's a remarkable sensation."

"All right. We're finished arguing. Stay or don't stay, it's up to you," I told him.

He could tell I just wanted him out of there. He said, "I'm not going anywhere with that man."

"Okay then, let's take the back door. It's nailed, we'll have to pry it."

"He'll hear us. He's listening."

"I'm taking the back door. I'm leaving."

"Well and good, then." He stood quite still.

Instead I hit my purse for the rum. "I don't see why I should have to leave," I said. "Nobody's after me."

"I'll have some of that," he said about my rum.

In a few seconds, I sat on the bed. "What did you *do?*"

He sat down beside me. "I told you. Didn't I? I can't remember what I've told to whom, by this time."

Among the two dozen noises coming in through the window, there were twenty I couldn't identify. That's where that raw feeling comes from when you're run up on a foreign shore—nothing's identified. You just can't take enough for granted. "You work for Watts Oil, you said. That doesn't make you a spy."

"I've given away the company's secrets."

"Right, you said that, but—doesn't your company sell gasoline? What's all the fury about?"

"We take petroleum out of the earth to keep everybody *alive,* for Christ's sake—it's the biggest game *going.*"

"But I mean anyway. How big a secret can your secrets be?"

"*Well,*" he said, "*listen,* the location of these things, deposits and so forth, I'm surprised at you, where do you spend your time that you don't know governments take a deep intertest?"

I was seeing it now. "You told Nicaragua something."

"I jolly damn well did, about the location of an oil deposit. A possible location."

"Possible? You mean maybe it isn't even there?"

"Testing's begun. That's the full extent of it. There may be a batch under Lake Nicaragua, and if it's there, it spills over into Costa Rica. Costa Rica already knew of it. Nicaragua had a right to the information, it seemed to me."

"So you blew it around, what a fool. And now this Costa Rican is after us."

"He's not after us. He has us."

An idea suggested itself: "I think we should kill him."

"*Do* you."

"Then we'd have his jeep."

"And his wallet and his trousers. And his body."

"We could put the body in the trunk."

"I don't believe that thing has a trunk."

"Are we speaking seriously about this?"

"Of *course* not," he said, "for goodness' sake. Do you know, I was warned about you. People said, Nicaragua, my God, there's a guerrilla war on, the place is full of killers. Only they meant *foreign* killers."

"Down here, we're the foreigners. We're the ones without any documents on file, no fingerprints, no relatives."

"I hadn't thought of it that way."

"We're alone, we can't be touched," I insisted, "we're dangerous."

"I'm not dangerous," he said. "I would never kill anyone."

"But you'd screw yourself all up. You'd get yourself in a corner way far away from home, wouldn't you? Spreading it around about oil wells."

"I had a notion everybody should start even."

"Start even, oh," I said, "now there's a notion that doesn't apply here at all."

Now he was crying about what he'd done to himself. "I told *them*," he said, "and *they* told Costa Rica that I'd fucking *told* them, you see."

He was waking up to it slowly. Gradually and enormously the dawn of all he'd done to himself . . .

"I could say anything right now," I told him, "and it wouldn't matter."

"Then *help* me . . ."

I'd done only one thing to help him—I'd tried to call him on the phone and warn him—but that one good deed had set me over the brink, and I felt myself slipping down with him . . . In order to stop helping him, I had to help him a little longer . . .

"They're sort of after me, too," I admitted, "at least to

the point where I don't want to talk to them, or him. Or anyone."

He didn't answer.

"We're a hell of a pair. You know what, I spend almost
every day doing nothing. Do you realize that? Once every two
weeks I get slightly off the wall. Why did you have to
coincide?"

He took out his wallet and started looking at all the things
in it, the business cards and identification cards and so on,
weeping.

There was no consoling him. "I suppose you love your
family and all that," I said anyway.

"Yes, yes, I do. I do love my family."

He cried without shame, like a girl . . .

What a fate!

Every time I turn around, they're jamming something
under somebody's fingernails, and I'm supposed to watch.

I HAD TO observe him. In fact they were upping my voltage, weren't the little demons, doing away with whatever was formerly unimaginable, putting before me for observation the most horribly tormented soul of all, the humanitarian among the damned—dressing him in a blue suit, grooming him presentably, handing him an appointment book . . . Believe me, looks deceive: among these souls he would have liked to help, with their diesel-blackened nostrils, their gnarled, arthritic hands and shrivelled guts, their faces rubbed away against the wheel of need, among these *he* was most definitely the pick hit, the big contender, the one to watch . . .

Next morning I got the Señora to unlock the phone for me. This equipment wasn't there for customer use, but the Señora never minded. She liked me—always looked away from me, smiling in a tight-lipped way. The General of Maids seemed fond of me, too. They didn't know who I was but they knew I wasn't holding any terribly high cards.

I needed to check on the Englishman's luggage. Also I had to find us another place to stay—where I was living now just wouldn't do anymore, decorated as its entrance was by the off-course policeman from Costa Rica. He seemed to feel at home here. At dawn he'd been stomping around out in the lobby, invoking childhood terrors. He answered to no one and nobody questioned him.

Even now this OIJ person watched me through the window, at the same time eating his breakfast of freshly sliced mango out of a little plastic bag. He sat on the fender of his jeep, eating with his fingers, leaning forward with his feet wide apart in order not to dribble on his shoes.

First I dialled the Inter-Continental, because it was just such a pleasure dialling the Inter-Continental: somebody always answered right away. But nobody of real authority ever wanted to get on and converse. The desk clerk transmitted dreams and legends as to when the manager might appear . . . Obviously I'd have to go over and find this manager myself.

The line started crackling in a jazzy fashion. Just before the telephone died, I got through to another motel and found us new accommodations.

Back in my room—*my* room—the Englishman was just in the process of smelling his shirt before putting it on for the third immolating tropical day . . .

I told him I was off to the Inter-Continental and served him a number of counterfeit assurances as to his luggage.

"Please, by all means, find me a pair of undershorts that aren't completely soggy," he begged.

The Costa Rican outside didn't budge or blink when I left, he just sat on his fender with his sunglasses parked on his scalp—a greasy habit that—committed, I supposed, to following the Britisher only.

I smiled at him, but I was faking it, I felt much more like crying . . . If only a self-admitted Costa Rican cop in Nicaragua had made any sense at all, I wouldn't have feared him quite so hysterically.

But while I looked for a cab, oh! the revitalizing surges of my economic status . . . These gypped Coca-Cola addicts heaving around the streets with their empty bellies couldn't help looking at me with a certain supernatural awe—financially, I was spectacular, miraculous; the minute I hit the pavement, the day's rivulet of cordobas started flowing from my hands . . . "Mother," the cabdrivers shouted, "soothe my coffers." *Mother*, the mutilated posters cried, *where they speak your name it says Money* . . . I intended to ditch my British friend today. But I wanted to stay with him, too, I liked being naked with him, the way he smelled made me feel both hungry and sorry, I liked knowing we were in for it, that we didn't have far to go . . . "Mother-I-am-penniless-it-hurts—intercede-for-me-in-your-mercy," the boys out front of the Inter-Continental pleaded. "Mother, let me go through your pockets," wept the desk clerk. What a morning! . . . If I'd been the fattest woman on earth, or blasting away with a bazooka, they couldn't have treated me with more respect . . . All but the doorman, who must have known me from the night shift, and failed pointedly to operate his equipment. Now it turned out that the fugitive manager had left a suitcase belonging to the Englishman, also a piece of his hand-luggage, in the hotel's travel office, right next to the desk of a lady who spoke English and didn't care whom I claimed to represent, if I wanted these bags I could take them. "Get a real job, you sorry fuck," I told the doorman by way of a tip, and dragged this stuff out front myself, and was carried off in my taxi with a trunk full of I didn't know what.

Having scored this luggage, I wondered should I steal it. Certainly it would have been the reasonable and prudent thing to do . . .

Halfway home the taxi's radio suddenly burst into song. False alarm, it died just as quickly.

"What's happening," the driver mumbled to himself, "am I going crazy?"

When I got back to the Englishman he was in a state of depression; it stood to reason: he was doomed.

"I got one suitcase and one little carry-on thing," I said.

He was just as gloomy after hearing this. "May I have a cigaret?"

"Yes." I gave him one.

"Cheers."

"Let's go, squire."

It was then that we left La Whatsis, where I'd lived for four months, and reenacted our ruses of the day before in order one more time to lose the accompaniment of the OIJ, and I introduced the Englishman to another of the sort of motel where a Watts Oil representative would never have stayed unless his life had gone absolutely to pieces. He didn't even ask where we were going.

I'VE ALWAYS been curious about the meaning of what followed. In its chief aspects the rest of the day was a price-slashed rerun of the day before. Maybe these things had to be done all over again on a reduced, murkier level. Every day I was taken to a more terrible region and made to reproduce my error.

Are there crimes I can commit that add to my indefinite sentence? Oh, blubbery invisible torturer, was it just that I hosted some short-lived idea of being of assistance? I didn't mean it. Please, I take it all back . . .

When I'd offered to help the Britisher lose this OIJ man with whom we'd since been reunited, I'd only been up for some entertainment, I hadn't really wanted to *help*. This I swear.

I swear that that uncompleted phone call, the one I'd tried to put through to warn the Englishman at his hotel the previous day, was my only action motivated by a sincere desire to help another. But for even such a tiny act of generosity as that, forgiveness is out of the question. I can only do it again, I think—repeating, in a series of rearrangements, that one mistake. And in scene after scene the Englishman, for his part, can only accept my assistance, which, as any fool but him can see, is *his* big mistake.

Yesterday we'd lost the OIJ man in the Mercado and hidden ourselves in a cheap motel; today we did the same . . . Like mechanical dolls in a clock, we pop out regularly and stage the same dumbshow.

There are two mercados, one is the Mercado Central, which we'd already experienced, and the other is the corrupt, awful mercado, an airless labyrinth of hawking and jewing, something out of the Middle Ages, worthy of the wildest, most herpetic Arab, composed of scraps and stench, shaded from the grinding weather by burlap and old plastic sheets. This is the Black Market, the thieves' market. The human stink, the heat, the suck and press of poverty, it erodes the senses, I've been trapped in there myself a couple of times, and each time within seconds the buzz of commerce started to reverberate like the cries of multitudes being strangled . . . To get there we had to follow a spiral route into the heart of Managua, avoiding various one-way streets and taking the long way around such buildings as TELCOR and the military hospital.

Just as we'd done the day before, we rode in our cab with the Daihatsu following along behind, but today our conversation was one-sided. The Englishman watched out the taxi's window but never said a word, steeped in such a funk I really thought I ought to just go through his pockets and depart. Today he took no interest in our policeman, whose unexplained presence and scary vagueness and all that were the whole reason for this move.

I told the Englishman he was going to repeat our mercado trick, only this time he'd do it by himself. He didn't object. Or indicate awareness particularly.

"There you go, hon," I said, shooing him out of the cab next to the small community of burlap and contraband. From without it had an element of the circus—wind-influenced roofing covering a grotesque throng, mysterious delights, abandon.

He went into an opening and, as soon as he passed into the shade, winked out like an apparition.

The Costa Rican got out of his jeep and walked right past me. He went in behind the Englishman by the same way.

I let the cab go and stood in the streetside swirl of pedestrians. They came at me smelling of peach pomade and sweat.

The temperature was monstrous, you could reach out and grasp handfuls of it, the top of my head cooked while my throat, in the shadow of my chin, felt cool by comparison.

Whether we actually eluded the Costa Rican wasn't the issue. The important thing was not to let the OIJ know where I was off to now; because unlike the rest of these citizens, most of whom appeared to be trying to ram through buildings with their heads or claw their way up into the sky, I was actually going places, I'd been visited with a plan of escape . . .

Across from the mercado, on a street I thought was called Embarcadero (I had to guess at that, because for no good reason the street names had been ripped off the poles in Managua), was a garage dealing in used cars. Nobody ever bought the cars, they only traded them back and forth with each other, trying to convince themselves they must be getting ahead.

Two cars were for sale today. One was impossibly expensive, but I made a down payment on the other one, a Volkswagen, in cordobas, promising dollars in traveller's checks when the machine was ready to travel—the man hadn't quite finished preparing it.

He was using the air-compressor hose to spray a poison-smelling mist all over the engine compartment, dribbling it from a bottle through the explosive stream of air.

I was fascinated. "What's happening?" I asked. "What's in your bottle?"

"Diesel," he said. "It makes the engine brilliant."

And what did it do for your lungs? It was impossible to breathe. FUUUUUZZZHHH, he gave it another dose.

"Does this car work? Is it a good car?"

"Yes, very good, the best."

"Is there anything wrong with it?"

"No, not at all," he said, "although many times it won't start."

"Isn't that bad?"

"It's not a problem. The car needs one sparking element."

"How long will that take? I require a car today."

That took him back a few paces, but he recovered quickly. "Don't be in a hurry," he advised me. "Maybe I can find the part this week."

"When you install the sparking element, will the car go?"

He hit me with a shot of English: "Yes. From regular gasoline." Full of regret, he shook his head. "Diesel, no."

"Is that bad?" We were back to Spanish now.

"It's very expensive."

Any kind of fuel would be expensive for us—we had no ration coupons and would probably have to resort to bribery. "Will you fill the tank before I take it?" I asked him.

"Yes," he said.

"Will a full tank get me to the border?"

"Which border?"

"I don't know."

"You'll get there and return with one tank of gas," he said.

"I'm not returning," I said.

"That's good for you," he said.

"Can I have it tomorrow?"

"I told you once before, don't be in a hurry. The documents, by themselves, will take several days."

"Screw the documents," I said in English.

"You'll have to get documents of ownership, and more documents to take it across the border."

I didn't think so. If it came to it, we'd eat the car and walk across.

"It's a very good car," he felt obliged to remind me.

"Have you driven it?"

"No, because it doesn't start," he said.

I GAVE the mechanic five thousand cordobas, one-tenth the car's price at the black-market rate of exchange, and now I owed him nine hundred U.S. dollars. For the nine hundred I was relying on the Englishman.

I hailed another cab. Bending over slightly to grab the door-handle of a taxi was my chief form of exercise, opening those doors and smelling that combination of spilt gas and dirty socks . . . "Go to the border of the mercado, there. Let's wait there for my friend."

While our vehicle cooked at the edge of the mercado's byzantine chaos, I sat sideways with the door open and my heels off, my feet on what passed for a running board, wiggling my toes.

The last time I'd been in there foul hands had touched me secretly and voices raked my ears until I thought they'd draw blood, harsh rock-n-roll prodded me along aisles mostly dirt, across patches of concrete speckled with the fluids and essences of hanging meat, past pairs of gentlemen squatting face-to-face, introducing their colorful bantam killer-roosters to one another, beneath the eyes of cartoon characters nailed to crosses and alongside members of my family starving in cages . . . Yes, I'm lying, but you get the idea . . . Yet when I picture the Englishman crossing it to find me on the other side, I imagine that it's like outer space in there . . . Around him everything is stock-still, deep-frozen, cold as dry ice to the touch, but he doesn't touch any of it. Gravity doesn't hold him. He travels feather-like through a brittle silence. The phony gasoline ration tickets flare into ash as he passes, the gutless counterfeit radios start to play—nothing stinks, everything's black-and-white . . .

All the same he emerged, after twenty more minutes, with his hair shellacked by sweat, big wet stains under his arms, breathing hard and squinting against the daylight, looking over his shoulder like a thief. Human after all. He'd impressed me mightily by turning into an international fugitive, but he was just like the rest of us, I suppose.

I shouted to him and he found me. He'd come to life, he could talk. "I'm desperate for a bath."

"What went on in there?"

"I think I lost him. We lost each other, more accurately. I nearly bought a fighting cock."

"That surprises me."

"I would have let the little fellow go," he said. "He appeared rabid. He wasn't all that friendly."

"They're not supposed to be nice."

"Still, he probably deserves a chance."

I was glad to see him a little happier. He'd need every bit of a sense of humor to laugh off our new residence . . .

We had reservations at a motel near Managua's southern

edge, a rooms-by-the-hour joint painted, every last inch of it, very purple. El Purpureo, I'd always called it. It was the shade of certain rhododendrons, not all that ugly if they'd only given it a wash. "They" were the potbellied owner with the humiliated teeth of a sugarcane addict, and his youthful assistant, who assisted him diligently in watching the TV. Not to suggest that I'd spent a lot of time at El Purpureo, but I knew that the television was just inside the front entrance, that it was made out of white plastic, and that the better part of their waking hours passed while they sat on wooden folding chairs beside a stack of half a dozen Fanta soft-drink crates, watching programs.

This is where they're always found. This is where the Englishman and I find them.

We're both tired, drained by constant fear, the unrelieved jimjams at a honking horn, at brakes squealing, at sounds imagined or anticipated—a footstep, a knock on the door. I just want to be forgotten by governments. The Englishman just wants a bath. The owner just wants to rent rooms by the hour.

Naturally the owner doesn't remember me, doesn't remember our phone conversation, asks himself if I'm really here in front of him . . . He scratches his head and ponders our intentions while I go through the whole plan again, as if nobody's ever thought of staying here all night before. "We want to stay a few days. But we'll pay by the hour," I suggest.

I hand him four hundred cordobas.

Right away the clouds part in his mind. "Your rooms aren't ready yet," he says. "Wait."

The Brit is now permitted to take a shower, and I to sit by the front entrance (clients mainly use the rear), between him and the boy—who turns out be his nephew—watching the tube. Managua's TV station appears to be devoted, at this hour, to live music, people strumming guitars and singing songs in which the words "Sandinista" and "Frente" crop up frequently. As its refrain, one song called "Libertados" uses the Frente slogan "No pasarán" . . . Our pimp landlord joins in on the final line, and he and his nephew burst into laughter. I point at him—"Sandinista?" "Sí," he says, "somos Sandinistas!" I point at myself—"No pasaró?" Whatever he says, using a lot of slang I can't unwrinkle, indicates that as long as I let drop a few cordobas around his establishment, I can pass anywhere, anytime.

He begins to cough raggedly.

Leading members of the Frente are standing before the television audience now, answering questions. But the nephew only snorts, and the landlord laughs and coughs.

Down here the elder folk really know how to produce a cough, they bring it up from the hips with a roaring like that of a Caterpillar tractor. I place a hand on my sternum, hoping he doesn't think I'm offering him my tits, and ask the old character if he's been to the clinic yet.

He indicates as best he can to the senseless gringa, pointing at Señor Ortega of El Frente Sandinista de la Liberación de Nicaragua who is speaking into the cameras, that if you get your fingers cut off at work in this country, you'll get no doctor, no compensation, no nada. I guess he's making some comparison to his lung trouble, but maybe he's misunderstood my question.

Shyly a boy and girl come through the front entrance, holding hands, and the old man escorts them to a room.

He's still coughing when he returns.

I have lived in a succession of stair-steps downward I believe. I have lived in St. Patrick's Day, a land of free green beer and screaming trains, and I have lived in Mardi Gras: Caucasian real-estate men in black-face and hula skirts dancing on restaurant tables . . . Down is the direction. But the scene never changes: there's a man, and I'm walking into a a motel with him, and the Night Person is there to accommodate us.

"Why can't we have a room?" I ask. "You had a room for them, didn't you?"

He watches the TV screen a minute. "Your rooms are still being used," he says.

THE ENGLISHMAN came downstairs, done with his soapless cold-water shower, looking pink as a cat's tongue. He hadn't been in this zone long enough to catch a tan on his face.

In a while the landlord took us up to our rooms.

We took a look at my room first, a purple region with a toilet, shower, sink, and bed all in the same twelve square feet. Overhead a long white malfunctioning neon tube waxed and waned and shimmered stroboscopically so that things happened to your mind.

We didn't get around to seeing the Englishman's room that day. As we stood in my doorway speechless, he put his hand on the back of my neck, and a most curious inner transition was accomplished . . . Almost on the order of a car wreck . . .

FROM THAT instant, whatever we did, all of it, counted as lovemaking, which seemed to have burst in upon two humans for the first time without wearing any of its disguises.

M I N U T E   T O   minute we couldn't remember what we said to each other. Words didn't count. We sat naked together under the cold-water shower for decades drinking from a pint of rum, while out in the streets the foreign sobs and laughter intimated symphonies, and we kissed to this accompaniment . . . The chorus had no words but "mm" and "oh" . . . One did the vowels, one did the consonants . . .

Sometimes I got tired of it. I'd trudge downstairs and watch television and let it build again, return to him and feel us, as we made love in that strobe-lit place, descending through room after room.

I'm telling you I was in deep, we both were, it was a honeymoon, that whirligig of crashing nuances and dismal reconciliations, vistas of hope redeemed, endless milliseconds free of natural law. We spent a night away from each other in separate rooms—I had nightmares of losing him and I found myself sitting on the edge of my bed at four a.m. Did you think I was going to say anything but a.m.? Do you want to talk about darkness? I loved him! Everything about him was candy. The vulnerability of his skin seized up my throat; sometimes I felt I couldn't live anymore. And so on . . .

"You're handsome."

"Are you kidding?"

"No, I'm lying . . ."

He was faceless. But he had a beautiful ass. His bottom was like an upside-down heart filled with the blood of martyrs. Would you think that about anyone you didn't truly love? I loved him! In my heart, my belly, in my bones, my teeth, I loved him!

He was in love with me too. In the morning I'd kiss him

in bed while the light came under the vented eaves. I'd feel his mouth around my tongue and the light slicing through my back, turning my lungs to gold; he liked to have me breathe into his mouth and out of his mouth. At a time like that there was only one of us.

But then I might get out of bed to go to the toilet, and suddenly we were two people without hope of ever understanding each other.

"I'm frightened of you. You make me afraid." We were so in love that he was tender and happy, even as he said these things. "You want me to think you're so terribly hard and cynical. But I know—you like to be touched, don't you."

"Maybe . . . By you . . ."

"You never smile." We kissed. "But your eyes are more kind than any I've ever seen."

I was glad I scared him. It made me feel less afraid.

Sometimes when I closed my eyes I saw a kind of shrunken, demonic but still beautiful if very white rendering of his face. Waking in the morning, I was launched into the universe where he was. Going to sleep, I passed into the dreamland he inhabited. The beginning and the end was in every word he spoke. I would look into his eyes sometimes and see my mother and father making love.

I don't know, *I* don't know . . .

"You have beautiful breasts."

"They're small."

"Your breasts are perfect, beautiful, perfect."

"No, they're too small."

"I refuse to believe that. To me they're perfect."

"But to everyone else, you mean, they're too small."

"Whatever size they are, I love them."

"You mean you think they're too small!" And I broke down weeping . . .

I can't remember what we promised one another during

that long, fitful evening interrupted by a handful of daytimes; I can't remember what we said, what we dreamed, what we witnessed, who we thought we were . . . But I remember with what passionate conviction I cherished the belief that I would never forget . . .

"You're a romantic. Are you a romantic?"

"Maybe. I surprise myself."

"You have a wife."

Now why did I say that?

"And two children," he said.

T H E P A R T for the car didn't come and didn't come. Nearly a week went by. We didn't mind.

One day as we were done making love, the sheet held a rusty stain in the shape of a tulip.

I dragged the sheet from the bed and ran cold water over the spot. He had to stand in the corner of the room as if he'd done something bad. "No, lie down," I told him. "We don't need a sheet every minute, do we?"

He lay back down on the bare mattress on which one more stain wouldn't be noticed. "Does that mean we're over for a while," he asked.

"What for? I don't care, as long as we don't send them down a lot of bloody bedding—that would be a little embarrassing, I guess."

"You really don't mind."

"I don't know. Should I mind?"

I wet the towel and left the sheet there in the sink while I went to the bed and wiped him off.

"You're gentle." And we kissed.

He was thinking about something and looking at the bloody towel.

"My wife . . ."

"Oh, no. Don't start," I pleaded with him.

"No," he insisted, "it's nothing, it's just that my wife, I was thinking, won't ever make love to me during her time. It isn't her way. That's all. I find it very—well," he decided, "I'm glad you let me, it's delightful."

"Good. Good."

He was different. He was quiet. He was thinking about his wife.

" SHE'S HALF German. She works for a solicitor's on High Holborn—a scrawny little suite of offices, everybody there appears very sad, if you ask me. She translates for them. I really don't know what she gets out of it. Her colleagues seem to . . . It's not as if we need the money she makes. Or actually I suppose the case is we need a great deal *more* than that. I honestly don't understand why she puts herself to the trouble. I'm afraid she's having an affair. And the children, you see, being raised by one sort of—*retarded* Scandinavian governess after another, teenaged. Or Irish, I remember we had one of those. Three years ago—or four, four years ago now, in fact—she had an affair with one of the men she worked with in a publicist's firm. We very nearly . . . But I believe, I believe that we've . . .

"The children," he said, "are five and eight . . ."

THEN IN the occasional fluorescent light one day I suddenly took sick. The toilet bowl became the center of my world.

I'd had it more than once up north in Matagalpa, the leftist nation equivalent of turista, called I suppose *engagista*. But it was a little different every time you got it, and who knew? Maybe this time it was really something speedy and fatal . . .

Naturally while the symptoms multiplied and elaborated on themselves, I was scared to death. There were intestinal things with the equatorial intensity of piranha-fish and killer bees, I might have one of those. I'd heard of a disease called leishmaniasis that I did not want to get . . . The diarrhea might have been that of snail fever, the stuffy head resembled meningitis . . . This enumeraton was cut short by complete delirium: Nothing was purple anymore . . . The walls turned a deep green-yellow . . . Everything was furry, in each object I looked at I detected a lurking metamorphosis. I was reduced to a passage, a tunnel, nothing else—we're always turning up at weddings and seminars, looking in the papers for a better job, forgetting entirely how like a hollow *rope*, an elementary *worm*, is our basic physical design . . . That worm tried to turn itself inside out, and then I was treated to what an irrelevant and unnoticed lot of tits on a boar the rest of me can become, all the attachments that seem more real than the simple devouring and emitting thing I really am. The horrible *smell*—the Englishman disappeared into his own region of the building; had I strength to waste I'd have felt embarrassed.

I reassured him whenever he came around to comfort me. By the time he went looking for help I was feeling the episode pass. As I say, I lived in the bathroom, where everything seemed to be gelatinously quivering, by now because of my exhaustion and not from delirium. I looked up in the flickering light and thought I made out the silhouette of my landlord standing in the doorway with the Englishman.

"I need a doctor," I said.

"Ha! Ha!"—meaning we'd already covered that one.

"Can't you help her?" the Brit asked. "She needs a doctor."

Coughing and clearing his throat at the same time, the landlord answered unintelligibly.

"He needs one too, the poor, fat pimp," I said.

Then just as suddenly I got well. I woke the next morning and the world wasn't yellow anymore but violet, beautiful, and fresh as if a gale had swept it clean. Belatedly Señor Landlord brought me a couple of small white pills and several big ones packaged in a strip of tin foil. I ate them all at once, and they didn't come back up, or rush along through.

Inside of seventy-two hours I'd starved down to a saintly, X-ray translucence. When I looked in the mirror I saw the black lips and gums of a smiling dog.

For two days I took no nourishment but Fanta colas . . . I drank them and walked all over downstairs, where there were clean wet sheets hanging in the high-ceilinged halls and sweetening the atmosphere pitifully with an odor of soap. The light from above fell through the vents in the eaves and struck these sheets in such a way that they absorbed the un-relieved purple of the hallway and gave it back as benevolence . . . Hanging there, curtain after curtain, turning the hallways into a series of wet, lilac rooms—I'd never seen any-thing so rapt, so holy and so frail, so completely terrifying . . . To think that in the center of a boiling sea of sweat, this teardrop cowered in its purity . . . Beauty, especially the angelic beauty of bedding being de-stained between fucks, is the most frightening business going in Inferno '84.

Except for clean sheets, this was a rough time. We still had a couple of days to wait through anxiously for our car. Days in which the press of realities emptied our honeymoon of its occult power.

I myself was in real trouble, that was one of the realities. I occasionally took time to appreciate that the Department of Defense was after me to lift my passport, thanks to my having been struck by altruism like lightning. And the Englishman never mentioned the life he'd placed in limbo by his half-assed benevolence, but sometimes, when I wasn't supposed to be seeing it, he wore a secret face bottomless with losses.

As the time came to leave, the lurking details snatched at us, the decisions we hadn't made—in the first place, which border would we cross? North or south?

"Not north," I insisted, "the roads are bad, and also that's where the war is. The administration is completely informal up there. I saw how they do justice up there—right by one of the main roads in Matagalpa, about three hundred yards from my cute little house."

"Matagalpa . . ."

"I saw somebody strung up."

"Strung up, you say."

"Yeah. They hung him—a Contra. Suspected Contra."

"You don't mean to say they *hanged* him?"

"They hung him or they hanged him, either way he shit his pants and died."

He was stunned. "Oh, what an ugly thing to say."

I supposed he was right. "Fuck you," I said.

WE DECIDED on the southern border, which was closer anyway and made more sense, as far as gasoline was concerned—but we didn't think about gasoline. We didn't think about anything practical.

Questions hovered and were never asked. Why head for Costa Rica when one of us was wanted in that country? Why not find a lawyer, or write a letter to the *Times*, or what about the Brit putting a call through to somebody he could trust at Watts Oil in London, or contacting a relative, even his wife?

These were considerations that turned up in the vicinity of our desperate little chats, but we never *considered* them.

I don't know about his, but my mind wouldn't think, it would only lift up horrible possibilities and shake each one at me like a club. Act! Run! Hide! Later you can be rational! We had problems here we couldn't cope with. Don't you get it? We didn't know where to begin! We had to erase ourselves from this map and pop up in the middle of another one like tunnelling rodents.

Still the car wasn't ready . . .

A N D   S T I L L we had those moments. I remember in particular calling out to him the last time we made love in our little room something like, "Cover me, oh, keep me covered . . ." One of those moments when it seems like something's going to work . . .

T H E   C A R was ready.

TWO

I'M STANDING out back of the Nicaraguan town of Masaya. A volcano sends up a cloud of steam in the distance . . .

Far off there's a black storm, full of lightning. Overhead it's clear. Two stars are already visible.

Looking out over the dusk-covered earthquake craters while the storm descends I think of another of William Something Merwin's lines: *The lightning has shown me the scars of the future* . . .

This was the end of our first day travelling. We'd turned off the highway, and while the Englishman went to Masaya's open-air mercado looking for God knows what, I wasted time.

Behind some kind of cultural center characterized mainly by stillness and an air of neglect, I leaned on a rock wall overlooking a volcanic lake and talked with a lady from a tour bus. I'd noticed her only last week at the equally deadly cultural center in Managua; she happened to be one of a group of musicians from Madison, Wisconsin, getting a taste of Third World socialism. Getting a bellyful. Like so many of us who'd descended into this region, she was a small bit horrified . . . What, no hot water, and I have to wipe my bum with words?
. . . We looked at Nicaragua stretching out toward wherever it went, the Pacific Ocean was a good bet. Whatever was going on down here, it was none of our business. Only she

couldn't admit it yet. Two minutes after our conversation I forgot what we'd said . . . The volcano spoke unmistakably. Everything else was a lie.

Wait a minute, it's coming back to me, she described herself as a player of the bass viola if I have it right, and we watched the moon go from an amber blob to a strong pearlescent light, along the lines of a smashed egg reassembling itself.

"I don't know. We're going to visit Jinotepe next," she said.

"I've been to Jinotepe. I think it has a lot of brick streets. But I can't remember," I said. "Where do you stay?"

"We stay at these little kind of like hostels."

The yellow moon came out from behind the volcano, travelling sideways fast, and surprised us. You had to go forty miles outside of Managua to find anything to see, but the effort paid.

"And what about your bass viola?" I asked.

"I don't know," she said, "what do you mean, exactly?"

The moon's face was just like the Englishman's. That's what I liked about him—his face was the moon's, I'd been seeing his face all my life, soft and not yet final.

"Well, do you carry it around with you? Are you guys giving concerts, I mean."

"No," she said, "no."

Her companions were getting on the tour bus—it was one of the modern ones having plenty of room and very small wheels.

"Well . . . There they are," she said.

"I wonder where my friend is? I've been waiting an hour."

"Are you with someone?"

I didn't like her asking questions. I didn't like anyone asking questions.

The fat-faced moon. The moon whose bow tie we can never see. The market should have been closed by now.

"Well," she cried, "I think that's a terrible remark to make!"

What had I said? Ah, something or other probably.

Then—was it him? He stood at the edge of the parking lot in a suit exactly the color of the dusk. You couldn't say for certain that he was real. He didn't come near. I didn't imagine it then, but probably he was already dead.

THE VOLKSWAGEN'S air-conditioner puffed out a fiery stink. We travelled with the windows down, serenaded by the psycho humming of the tires, which were retreads from some socialist workers' paradise across the sea. When we got up a little speed the wind thudded around our heads—and the temperature stayed right up there, but it wasn't as sticky.

Women idling on one leg, like storks, with the sole of one bare foot clamped against the other knee, stood looking up and down the highway . . . As in every region, rivers with the names of animals, streets with human names, places eternally irrelevant, landscapes as innocent as water in cupped hands. Billboards swung by trying to tell us things—No Pasarán—FSLN—red hammer and scythe over the Communist Party's initials, MAP-ML—CASTROL GX—ALTO—and on the poles and walls were posted various exhortations and explanations ("There are no replacements because everything must go to the defense of our country"—et cetera, I forget the rest) . . . Desperate surviving made comprehensible through torn slogans . . .

Pulling to the side of the road we would survey the scene

and check out the roadside pedestrians, looking for the face that might have half a brain behind it. And then we'd ask our questions. I've experienced starvation and thirst, but never the drained, aching need for information, anything, the smallest piece of data—left or right? near or far? open or closed? is there a garage? a constabulary outpost? a meal? a drink? what time? how far?—that powered our movement along the edges of those towns. I got so that I trusted most the mean-looking jungle farmers trudging along by the road with their straw cowboy hats and machetes and hard brown flat bare feet like shapeless boots; but they were just as dumb as the others, completely in the dark as to what I was asking but not in the least reluctant to dish up an answer, giving me directions to places that will never exist, in colloquial phrases complicated by something they always seemed to be chewing, or sucking, and contradicted by their sign-language: a mix of rabbit-punches-in-reverse and caresses enacted on the air.

But don't think we covered a lot of ground on this trip— the entire ride happened on a hundred-mile stretch of the Panamerican Highway and some of its tributaries. The reason it took five days was that we didn't know what we were doing. We didn't know whether the border represented escape or danger, and so we dawdled in towns like Masaya and Rivas— the latter only twenty miles or so from the border—hoping to learn how to get across.

Rivas was set up just like Masaya and most other towns in Central America . . . The streets emanated from a court-yard and a tall cathedral raised by Indians under the lash of zealous padres many centuries ago, before the Indians acquired uniforms and automatic rifles. The farther you got from the central church square, the more haphazard grew the system of Moorish lanes, until you were likely to wander the rest of your life among high walls spangled with bullet-holes if you didn't have a map.

But Rivas's geography was simple enough. On one side of town was the highway, on the other a couple of red earthen roads that toddled a tiny distance toward the horizon before being pounced on and eaten by the jungle.

Except for the fact that I was born without any sense, I might have lived there in Rivas forever. In the first place, we found a motel in that town that accepted my cordobas—a *nice* motel, with toilet paper, soap, showers, small blue electric fan on the bedside table, a bar full of rum and a restaurant that served chicken and fresh cow's milk. On top of that, there weren't any police or Department of Defense people around. Soldiers staffed the local FSLN headquarters, but they weren't *after* anyone, they only liked to sit out front under the crimson-over-black slashes of the FSLN banner waiting for a capitalist revolution. The rural south of Nicaragua, if you asked me, was altogether genteel.

We woke up in the morning with the blue fan cooling us—because now the Englishman and I slept together always, trying not to touch because of the heat, but wanting to be near—and I thought to hell with it, this is absolutely the last motel, the last wadded Kleenex, the final ashtray. Let's just die here.

"Are we in a hurry?" I wondered.

"There you have me. It just may be we're not in anything at all—if you get my meaning, because I'm not sure I do myself."

"No. I get it. I agree."

"And so then, cheers," he said.

He wasn't happy. But couldn't I change all that with love? It was one of those moments again . . . Nothing so sad as the heart that cries, I can change, I can change! But we made love, and he went back to sleep . . . The Englishman did his sleeping in the mornings. And he was always able to sleep soundly in a moving car.

But he didn't sleep at night, because he didn't drink enough rum.

I did. I drank a little in the mornings—to wake up—and I drank a lot in the evenings—to sleep.

Oh well . . . Thus anointed I kind of coped. My poor Englishman drank only grief and fear, and he was drunk enough on that.

But he managed to rest a little every morning, and he was cheerful when he came out three hours later. It was good he was in shape to be reasonably sociable and gracious, because I wasn't alone.

I'd gone for a walk, and when I'd come back into the restaurant I'd found an American sitting there all by himself, a young redheaded man wearing round rimless sunglasses; he had a cute little red beard, too.

He invited me to watch him eat breakfast—how could I have turned down a chance to observe?—and told me all about the wonderful places he'd experienced on this, his first trip to Central America for the consulting firm by whom he seemed to want people to think he was employed.

He was eating a beans-eggs-rice collision called *gallo pinto* —a Costa Rican dish, the first instance I'd seen of it here in Nicaragua.

From the sound of things, a whole extended family was building an ark out in the kitchen, but no one came out to wait tables. We were the only customers—it was a dead place because it required money, and you can bet nobody in that town had any.

"Was that ABC Consultants," I asked him, "or did you say XYZ?"

He just laughed.

What did I know, I could never keep track of all the initials stamped on the documents and stencilled all over the buildings—P.S., Partido Socialista, MAP-ML, don't ask me what that stands for, FSLN, don't forget OIJ, and in the *Barricada* headlines for the last three days running: CIA.

He told me, "Look, these businesses—you should have seen the place we stayed at in San José. There was a swimming pool outdoors and another one indoors, there was a gambling joint right in the building—a casino, you know, with all that green felt. The outdoor pool was just for decoration. You can't swim in that cool weather, it's in the mountains. They have all kinds of money, these outfits we consult for; I mean the budget can be—you think these countries are poor, but it's only the *poor* people who are poor . . . We stayed at a mansion in the hills about a month ago, really an unbelievable spot, all we were doing was putting together an assessment on this one outfit, the owner put us up. The company president."

He had a sad, worried look about his face as if he thought he'd be misinterpreted or disbelieved.

"And what was the full name of this company you work for?"

"We're out of Connecticut, consulting is a weird game— to spell it out, businesses and industries hire us because they don't trust their own interpretations of their own data, and frankly, it's ridiculous what they pay. It's just silly. I'm not kidding, like right now I'm working on a report and if I need something I snap my fingers, like if I needed to hire you to consult for *me*, if there was something I needed you to do for me, I could drop an envelope in your lap with, what?—God, I don't know—it'd be easy as hell to scrape up about a thousand. A thousand U.S. I'll tell you, they don't let me sling around that kind of money up in Hartford. I don't stay with any company presidents up there, either."

Considering the pace of his mindless lying, it was quite a trick that he got any food in his mouth at all.

He'd finished his breakfast by the time the cook came out

from the kitchen, through a door behind the bar, and assembled himself before me. Defending his right to be a waiter, as it were. I pointed at the consultant's empty plate. "The same. And coffee. And half a glass of rum."

"It gets me," the consultant said when the cook was gone, "how everybody down here seems so impolite. Like the way you just ordered your food."

"Impolite?"

"Nobody says please or thank you." Suddenly an aching homesickness shone out of his face.

Now we talked about every part of the United States of America we'd ever either of us set foot in.

"I believe I'll have some rum and papaya juice," he told the cook when I received my breakfast.

"Who are you consulting for down here? Why on earth would anybody want to do business with the Sandinistas?"

"It's not the Sandinistas. Central America—this whole area is a gambler's paradise. Everybody's down here giving the odds a shake in whatever game they feel like playing, basically —in all seriousness, there are *wheat* conglomerates looking around down here, can you fathom that? Transportation people, resort people, oil interests, you get the picture. But anyway, I mention oil, my report happens to be about some aspects of the petroleum outlook, or the principal part of it concerns petroleum—matter of fact, your friend gets a little ink, even, I mean the guy you're traveling with, if he's the same person I'm thinking of. But—I'm not saying anybody wants to move their whole operation here, that's not what I mean, but the local business people are serious and levelheaded, we've got a strong administration up north, and we realize now that we can risk investments in the region because we already have a stake in Central America, we're committed here, and so on and so on," he said, giving the last few words a certain resonance by raising the glass and saying them into his drink.

The fact was, he couldn't do anything to us. If he was an American, then he was just as lost as we were.

"What do you mean, about my friend?"

He wore a cheap watch and a class ring from someplace. He had that fair redhead's skin—like the Englishman's—permanently blushing with the heat, nicely mated to his blue summer sports shirt with the sweat bleeding through.

"He's one of the characters," he said. "Haven't you noticed? All these entrepreneurs are kind of boiling around down here, and at the same time, you can't fail to notice, there's a strong and violent proletarian movement well launched in El Salvador, entrenched here in Nicaragua, brewing in Belize and also Guatemala. And in order to feel more secure, the most paranoid entity in the hemisphere, you know who I'm talking about, it *must* do everything in its power to mess up the balance around here."

"You mean the U.S."

He looked at me, quite obviously baffled. "God!" he laughed. "Why don't you stop being ridiculous? I mean the Castro government in *Cuba*. They have to do whatever they can to fuel the proletarian movement. It's the only way Castro can keep from sinking."

"What's this got to do with your report? And what do you mean by bringing up my friend?"

"All this has a lot to do with my report, because the report is about this region. And balance is what this region is all about."

"But what has your report got to do with my friend?"

"There he is. He's heading this way."

The Englishman had just come into the restaurant and paused at the bar to get a drink.

"What has your report got to *do* with him, I asked you."

"Like I say, I don't even know if it's the same guy." He tried to disarm his next statement with a laugh: "He wandered through and received scrutiny."

The Englishman probably heard this but didn't know it referred to him as he pulled up a chair and sat down.

"The Central American countries go on searching," my host resumed, "for *their* best way, not necessarily Castro's, not necessarily ours, a series of political experiments conducted under military restraint. Always held in check by the military. That's not our style, but it's theirs, so why not?"

"Why not indeed?" the Englishman said just to be participating.

"But what do I know?" our consultant friend said.

"You probably know whether or not to recommend the food," the Englishman suggested.

"If you're hungry, get some—it's pretty good, not bad at all."

"Rather simple fare, I noticed."

"You mean—on the menu?" the consultant said.

I said, "It's the first gallo pinto I've seen. We're getting closer to Costa Rica."

"So, are you guys heading for C.R.? What goes on for you down there?"

"Nothing special, as I understand it," the Englishman said.

"The menu gets better," I said.

"But not the rum." This was the consultant's conjecture, as he looked down into his glass. Although he was the phoniest human I'd so far met in the flesh, he slugged back his liquor with a satisfaction that couldn't have been faked. "What other good stuff can I expect up here?" he asked.

"Have you been around Managua much?"

"I've only been here one day, tell the truth."

"Well, they don't have anything up there. The cities can't cope."

"None of the stuff they have in Costa Rica? No coffee? No sopa negra?"

"Sopa negra!" I agreed. "I love it!"

"And what's *that* made of?" the Englishman asked. "Sounds fascinating." He hadn't touched his drink.

"Black beans. Turtle beans," the consultant told him. "Don't they have it up here in Nicaragua? Black soup?"

"Only in the sense," the Brit said, "that it seems to be all around us."

"I'm not surprised." The consultant was knowing. "Their socialism doesn't work. They've got the biggest army going," he announced, "and not one turtle bean."

Now we had a stupid silence, the kind that always descends on people who are half in the bag.

"I've been down in San José for about the last—almost a month," the consultant said.

"Do you ever get over to the Key Largo?" I asked him.

"*That* place? It's a whorehouse."

"It's got a sort of entertaining ambience," I submitted in its defense.

The Englishman took the wheel. "And have you ever been to England."

The redhead answered, "My mother is from England."

"Oh, what a coincidence. But then we're all cousins, I suppose, if you seek back far enough in the history of things."

"I'm sure we're very closely related," the American said.

The Englishman's breakfast came along, and he ate it, although he seemed to be suffering silently, especially when a reckless feeling came over me and I started talking about my trouble with the Central American money market.

I was onto the rum and papaya juice now, a grisly concoction, overly sweet.

They probably wondered, the both of them, what the hell I thought I was doing. I held forth bitterly on the subject of the war in the northern provinces and then got on to bad-mouthing the Vice-minister at Interturismo, the man who'd helped me find lodging for cordobas instead of dollars.

The redhead laughed a lot and kept interrupting with requests for more details, for clarification, for first and last names.

The Brit signalled me horribly with his eyes.

"Don't worry," I told him right in front of this alleged consultant, "he knows all about us anyway."

But my Englishman looked even worse, as if his foot were being crushed and he mustn't scream, when the redheaded man claimed to have an arrangement to sell cordobas across the border for Costa Rican centimes and I said, "Oh, really."

"We're all agreed, Nicaraguan money stinks," the consultant explained. "I wouldn't have bought any in the first place if I didn't have someone to sell it back to."

"You can almost always sell it to some black-market person or other right at the border," I said, "the Costa Rican side. Anyone can."

"I can get you a better rate."

"I'm surprised to hear that. But somehow not totally astounded."

"Forgive me for changing the subject," the Englishman said, his fingers squeaking on his wet glass, "but the elections rather interest me. I wonder if there's a newspaper . . ."

From the consultant he got the same look of naked incomprehension he might have by announcing a passion for people's unwashed feet. "I guarantee you this," the consultant said finally, "if we kept stalling on elections like these guys— in the U.S., I'm saying—somebody would overthrow the government."

With palpable relief the Englishman started arguing otherwise. Latins were accused all too easily of procrastination, it wasn't quite fair, et cetera. Certainly, the elections were slow in coming by *current* U.S. standards. "But think back to your own revolutionary era—between your insurrection and the election of this fellow George Washington, didn't nearly seventeen years elapse? At a comparable stage in the birth of a new Nicaragua, the Sandinistas actually turn out to be quicker off the mark by nearly a dozen years, don't they?" He wiped his mouth unnecessarily with his napkin and transmitted various subtle pre-flight signals. "Why don't you and I take a stroll around town," he said to me, "maybe we can locate a paper. It's got quite a Spanish feeling, the town, don't you think so?" he said to the consultant, moving back in his chair.

"Give me a minute," I told him, "I'm thirsty."

I ordered something cool.

"Ah." He sat there with his chair pushed away from the table, and crossed his arms.

Something seemed to turn over a bad card in the consultant's head. "Not that free enterprise is much better," he said out of nowhere. "Down here . . ."

He looked at the Englishman and said, "Whores, is what they all are."

"I—*beg* your pardon?"

"I mean they'll all do it for enough money, any of these women, Costa Rican, Venezuelan, I'm not kidding in the least. Grab one coming out of church sometime and try it. You'll see what I mean. They're all lonely as widows, that's the real truth about them, they haven't had a man's hand on their thigh since Jesus was in diapers. Sure, I've been around the Key Largo, and I couldn't tell what part any of those people were supposed to be playing, the men *or* the women. In the end I'd say, if you've got some money to lose, put it down on a horse race or something and go back to the hotel and play with yourself." We laughed at this and he concluded with a remark that seemed to float before us, "The area is full of amateurs."

Then he rode right over it: "So who's this minister down there you were saying? You don't mean a *preacher*? You said, yeah, a vice-minister or something? What was his name?"

"I have a terrible head for names."

"He was in the tourist department, or what exactly did you say?"

"You are, I mean, *unbelievably* obvious."

"I could probably get you in touch with my bankers. You don't sell your money to the characters right at the checkpoint there. You go all the way into La Cruz—you know it? Yeah? I think they call it that because it's nothing but a crossroads and four petrol joints. Two of them are closed anyway."

"I was through La Cruz on my way up here."

"I'm going for a paper," the Englishman said.

"Look, okay, I'll set this thing up, I think I can do it."

"Nobody asked you," I said.

"If you want, I mean."

"I really have to be going now I think," the Englishman said.

He'd committed himself, he got up from his chair. But I didn't leave with him: because I felt he was pushing me, he didn't trust me to keep out of trouble—because he refused to trust me.

The consultant watched him go without saying goodbye. "He's not an American. He's definitely British, right?"

"You tell me."

"Yeah. But who is he to you, exactly? How long have you known him?" He laughed like a kid. "Well, listen to me!"

"I don't mind listening but I don't feel like answering, you know?"

"Is his passport for real?"

It's a mystery how he managed to beat me over the head with these questions and at the same time make me laugh at the very fact he thought he could get away with asking them . . .

I told him I'd been with Eyes for Peace. Helping to maintain the integrity of borders in a troubled universe . . . He was contemptuous. The Sandinistas had no future: "Except for the intense involvement of the Castro government and the indirect—in some cases direct—involvement of the Russians, the Central American proletarian movement isn't a permanent consideration."

Oh no no no. Not at all. In fact, they'll all be gone in a minute or two . . . "Only rum is forever," I agreed.

"In the long stretch the movement's a volley in the Ping-Pong game between the rich and the poor down here, it might result in certain corrections, in many respects it won't amount to anything, possibly we'll live to see it pass on, die out, and sometime in the future flare up again. *Unless* Castro extends his influence and deepens the socialist entrenchment in the politics of the region. In that case we're not talking about proletarian agitation with a constructive outcome. We're talking about trained-up Cubes walking all over the toys down here. If Castro has his way too much longer, this whole area's going to be unbalanced for centuries, and our own country maybe gets mixed up in a war."

He went in a giant dizzy leap from the general to the personal. "What were you doing back when Vietnam was showing every weeknight on the tube? Demonstrating against it on a college campus?"

"I'm not *that* old. How old do you think I am?"

"I think you're about thirty and I know you're not *that* old, excuse me. I watched that war on TV every night because my older brother Rick lived in Vietnam at the time, in the jungle, out of a pack—he was a U.S. Marine. He lived there—on the front lines of the same conflict that's going on down here. And he died there."

False sincerity always makes me sweat with embarrassment. In what he was saying there were far too many burned-out words. But he was compelling, his Adam's apple plunged and leapt, the tendons of his throat jerked taut as he hoisted these drowned ideas above the froth . . .

"I have a younger brother, Charlie, who's still alive. I don't want Charlie to spend his last few minutes spitting blood and trying to stay on his feet by hanging on to that tree out there by that wall, or some other tree just like it somewhere else in Nicaragua. I have a right to care how it all turns out down here. It relates to my family. I'm really fucking pissed at anybody who fucks with the arrangement.

"How do you know this British guy? I can tell you don't go back too far. I can see it in the body language. How do you know he *is* who he *says?* How do you know he's not a—whatever, you fill that one in, somebody you hadn't counted on, could be anybody, is the point I'm making. And, hey—*I* know how exotic it can feel down here, every connection is ten volts higher—when I meet a dark-eyed lady down here I don't ask for references. So you didn't ask for references. That's not a crime, that's a mistake. And mistakes can be corrected."

Another absurd fuckhead.

"Do you know how crazy you are?" I asked him.

"I've put you in the picture. I've let you know what you can do by helping me with my report, and I've let it fall out where I stand, and that's only fair, anyway that's what *I* think."

"Are you clinically insane? You're *really* nuts, really. You never said anything about helping you. Your memory is all messed up."

"Wait a minute, will you? We're just sitting around getting sloshed because it's Sunday, okay?"

"It's more like Tuesday or Wednesday. It isn't Sunday."

"Okay, you win. Now, do you want to change the subject? I'm bored." He smiled one of the most charming smiles I've ever seen and called in Spanish across the room, "I'm ready to drink! Can we have some rum?"

We had a couple, and after a point I said, "To live outside the law you must be honest."

"There you go."

"You don't know what the fuck I'm talking about."

"I'm faking it," he admitted. "I'm not honest. I don't live outside the law."

It was torture to feel him doing trial-and-error on me, seeking the key word. "There isn't any key word," I said out loud. "All your words are burned out."

"I know that," he said. He was a goner. Giant blue circles under his eyes—with that hair of his, his head, wouldn't you know, was red, white, and blue . . . He looked across at me from the other side of a cloud. "Don't you think I know the words don't work?" he said.

Histrionically he raised up his two hands before us. "I see trained-up Cubes walking all over the toys. Let's be realistic, those are the choices, us or them. If I can change that, tell me how, tell me how, I'd give anything—but just be realistic."

"All right, I will be. Anything for a friend, hey?"

"Look, I don't know what you think of me," he said. "I was just offering about this deal, I mean it's the *only* deal I could set *up* across two *borders*—I've only *been* here two weeks . . . It's for real, and it's straight."

"Just what exactly is this deal," I said, "better fill me in, I've lost track."

The sale of my cordobas, that was the arrangement he'd supposedly been making. He himself had forgotten. "How does it feel to you," he ventured. "What kind of deal do you think is being offered?"

"I think you're offering to screw me," I said with fatigue and also, I admit, with some interest.

"That's the one thing I'm not offering to do, no."

"What. You wouldn't mess around with a lady like me?"

"Not on an afternoon like this. But I'd sure buy you a drink."

Until right now his fairy propensities hadn't manifested themselves.

I got up. "Excuse me—is that polite enough for you?—I have to piss." Whether on purpose or not I don't remember, I toppled my drink so it dribbled in his lap.

That click had occurred in my head, that click after which you're no longer having a good time.

"What were you gonna do?" he said, wiping at his thighs with a napkin. "How do you get across the border? Wave a U.S. flag and gather up a few Contras?" As I left him he called, "What's the plan?"

I WAS dead to the world by five that afternoon and woke up in the middle of the night. I guess the rain coming down had awakened me.

Now I was moving onto the Englishman's rhythm of sleep—he was up, too, sitting by the desk, naked, but with a towel draped over his lap, hanging his head, the saddest man I'd ever seen.

"Is that son of a bitch still around?" I said.

"Who do you mean, the American?"

"What time is it?"

"Quite late. Or early."

"Let's leave, okay? Let's just get out of town."

"How can you get totally drunk, and then even want to get out of *bed*? Much less leave town?"

"I need to feel like I'm *getting* somewhere."

"They've got the car locked behind the gate, you realize."

"Well Christ, let's wake them up, let's just—"

The management had locked the car in the yard for safe-keeping. We couldn't get away. But having him awake was a comfort. The panic began leaving me. Whatever I feared, if it hadn't happened by now, it wouldn't happen till morning.

I lay back. "Are you mad at me? I mean I know you are, but I mean to the point of murder, let's say, that mad."

He came over to the bed and kissed me.

"Are you all right?" he asked.

"Yes. I don't know what's my problem. Sorry."

B U T—the Englishman . . . I didn't quite get around to telling him about that afternoon's drunken conversation. The American was my own problem. This trouble belonged to me. It was up to me to cope with it. And it's also true that I felt more comfortable having something over on my lover, if you understand what I mean, it was good to have compartments he wasn't privy to, right and proper to set up these barriers excluding him because, when you think about it, he didn't belong in my game in the first place, did he?

T H E   N E X T day en route to the border one of our tires went flat. We'd only gotten a mile out of the town of Rivas. "And the spare is flat too," I wagered.

"There isn't a spare," he said, banging down the lid of the trunk.

"We're dead. We'll pass out in this heat."

"We've only come two kilometers at most, wouldn't you guess? Are you willing to walk with me? I don't like leaving you here."

I felt feverish, queasy, and absolutely parched walking along behind him. It was actually overcast, but the air was baking.

He was surprised that I carried my shoes. "I walked barefoot all over Managua," I told him. "The night I first met you I walked all the way home barefoot."

"And was that somehow in my honor."

"Yeah. Kind of. I don't know."

The clouds seemed so much blacker in that part of things. You'd think the war was raging just past those hills, and the smoke of destruction covering up the sky.

At the garage in Rivas the young men were very kind as they begged us for money "as a souvenir," and picked out for us another wonderful pseudo-tire from Leningrad. One of them shouldered a jack and started off toward the highway, elatedly rolling the tire along ahead of him, until the others stopped him and gathered everything, and us, and them, into a pickup truck.

The closer we got to the car, the higher the price of this tire we were carrying. By the time we unloaded it you'd have believed it was made of heroin or ambergris, its value had swollen that much, and I had to be held back by the Englishman from strangling the larcenous little shits.

"We have the money," he insisted, "and they seem to have the tire, don't they."

"But they *said* two thousand!"

The young men worked casually but managed to get the tire installed, at a price of seven thousand cordobas, before any of us realized it didn't match the size of the other three.

But for no extra money at all they went back and got another and corrected their mistake, cheerfully and very slowly.

For that reason we had to approach the border at night. One of the tire artists insisted the border was closed by five p.m. every day, a policy instituted since the Contras, coming across the Río San Juan from Costa Rica, had blown up the kiosk and killed several guards three months ago.

The others said the guards weren't afraid of anyone and the border would be open whenever we reached there.

If it was open, that would guarantee nothing about the Costa Rican side of things. We might have to spend the night caught between two nations. And the Costa Ricans had to match the Nicaraguans in everything, so theirs was a system just as elaborate, with stamps, forms, payments, searches, defumigations at one point after another—I'd crossed over this border on my way in, and even before La Cruz the checkpoints began, about a dozen useless ones employing various bastard offspring and idiot relatives of all the politicians, right down to the most doubtful cousin of the least postal clerk.

We headed for the border in the dark. Ours was the only car on the road for the last thirty kilometers. There were no more towns, no more houses. The highway seemed to be a tunnel cut through a world of tree-tall grass, the picture in front of us was changeless, and except that I had to turn the wheel a little this way or that way to keep in the center of it, I'd have thought the car was standing still. At one point, a white Brahma bull was suddenly floating in the road ahead of us . . . And although my foot reflexively found the brake and we stopped, with the hood just beneath its drooling face and the screech of deceleration stifled instantly by the darkness, I couldn't quite accept this apparition. In a few seconds it was gone.

As we got closer to the border, the rain of tiny gnats off

Lago de Nicaragua obliterated the windshield. And it was no use turning on the wipers, because dead bugs aren't wet . . . And then I nearly drove through a cable stretched across the road. We'd come to the first border checkpoint. There wasn't a light on anywhere. A blinking, terrified soldier approached us.

"I've made a terrible mistake," I said.

The guard talked to us while other soldiers turned out of their beds and ambled through the headlights without shirts, shoes, or rifles to lean on the car, breathing and stinking. The border was closed.

I recognized one of the soldiers, a suffering entity who had looked at me with such venom, when I'd crossed five months ago coming the other direction, that his hatred had hummed a song in my ears and I'd distinctly felt it scratching at my skin . . . He said nothing tonight.

They all talked us over for a while. "Your passport."

I handed it through the window with a hand that wouldn't stop shaking.

"The passport of your comrade?"

"Oh, God, do they want my passport?" He handed it to me and I put it out the window. They handed the documents around among themselves and looked at them pointlessly and then gave them back. "Tomorrow at seven," the guard said.

We turned around and didn't say a word until we were out of sight of them.

At which point I stopped the car. My hands felt so rubbery I couldn't grip the wheel.

"What now?" he said quietly. "Back to Rivas I suppose."

I started to cry. "We could try Granada," I said.

"That's quite a ways beyond Rivas, isn't it?"

"We've got more than half a tank left." I cried some more. "I really don't think I'm going to make it, honey. I just feel like killing myself to get out of here."

He was quiet for a while.

I couldn't see him at all in the dark. Beyond the road the frogs and insects roared steadily.

"This car is filling *up* with these things," he said finally, slapping at gnats. "Do you feel well enough to drive on?"

W E S A W no one until we were halfway to Rivas. And then three soldiers with their rifles at port arms suddenly showed up in the headlights, boldly blocking the road.

They were hardly more than children. The spokesman, who'd ripped the sleeves off his blouse and wore a bandana around his neck, was both shy and demanding. He draped an arm on the car's roof and hung his head right down in my face.

They were doing sentry duty at a bridge up the road a ways, he explained.

"What do they want?" the Englishman said.

"They want a ride."

"Get in, get in," he said, gesturing invisibly at them in the dark, "just, please, don't do anything," he said, "to hurt us."

"Your country?" the boy said when they were all in the back seat and we were moving.

"Sweden," I said.

"Turn soon."

"The bridge isn't on the highway?"

He didn't answer.

"What's the trouble?" the Englishman said.

"I'm getting really scared."

The Englishman didn't want to talk about it.

"Here. Now we'll turn left," the soldier said.

"Is the bridge on this road?"

"Go farther."

The road became dirt following a mile or two of blacktop.
"Exactly where is this bridge?"

"Go farther. We have to guard the bridge against the Contras."

We ended up in San Juan del Sur, on the Pacific Ocean, forty-five minutes later.

"What type of place is this?" I asked.

The soldier with the necktie explained it had formerly been a tourist resort.

When the boy said this word, I said, "Well, a resort." It sounded nice.

"Is it a town?" the Englishman said. "It certainly appears to be a settlement."

"He says it used to be kind of a vacation resort."

As soon as we let them out, just before the bridge, they told us to get out of town.

"This is a bad place for Europeans," the spokesman explained.

"We're going to be driving all night. We're just getting more and more nowhere," I told the Englishman.

"I have an idea. Why don't we ask them politely to let us cross?"

All courage failed me. "You ask them."

He beckoned to the soldier, leaning toward my window, and called, "Por favor? Sí? Por favor?"

When the boy came around to his side, the Englishman kept on saying just those words, but laid his cheek against prayerful hands to indicate "beddy-bye" and then gestured across the bridge at the town, "Sí? Por favor?"

"Okay, okay."

"That's very kind of you, very kind . . ."

The boy waved us on and we passed over the wood bridge with a clumping sound, you'd have thought we were on horseback, and on into ugly San Juan del Sur.

It was after eleven. A lot of people were going home from somewhere. Silhouettes sprang up in the headlights. But it was hard to appreciate that they were substantial.

The town seemed only half-built. We bumped along dirt streets with nearly impassable gutters hacked right across them . . . They were certainly conserving on streetlamps in San Juan del Sur. There was nothing but a dusty, windblown dark that seemed to suck up, even before it hit the street, the light spilling from the occasional canteen or *soda*.

The FSLN office was open and brightly lit.

We drove by a pool-hall full of soldiers, and then along a row of stores and small houses; their unpainted facades gave the town an ambience of frontier remoteness. The streets weren't set around a church square in the usual style.

We found what must surely have been the only bar in town, a giant place with a blue dance floor, and a jukebox reverberating cavernously, but there was nobody in it other than the bartender and a little boy.

"Don't the soldiers and sailors come in here?" I asked them.

The bartender was tight-lipped. "Don't know."

"Can we eat something?" the Englishman asked in English, shovelling his hand toward his mouth.

We had chicken, rice, and coffee, and the bartender's whole family came out to get a look at us: two more smiling, happy kids, a smiling happy uncle or some such, a smiling happy woman who identified herself as the bartender's wife and as the author of our meal. The jukebox across the dance floor blasted Elvis's rendering of "Farther Along":

> *When death has come*
> *And taken our loved ones*
> *Leaving our homes*
> *So lonely and drear*

Then do we wonder
How others prosper
Living so wicked
Year after year

They directed us toward the town's only worthwhile hotel, and we started driving all over looking for it. As in Managua, the townspeople were getting along without street signs.

At one point the Englishman made me stop the car and back up in the street.

He flung his hand toward an open doorway and said, "Look there, look there," referring to two men in grey—were they wearing ushers' uniforms?

"Oh, Jesus Christ," I said. "Russians." The two of them sat before the counter of a *soda*, flanked by distinterested patrons, and mopped their faces and looked a million miles toward home.

"Officers," the Englishman said.

"Russian officers," I repeated. The sight of them absolutely disoriented and frightened me.

"Have you never seen a Russian person before?"

In my homeland, I might have told him, we're trained to rank the presence of uniformed Russians with the coming of the Kingdom. "They're not supposed to be real," I said.

"And yet there they are," he said. "Helping, I could very easily add. Meanwhile, the representatives of your government are somewhere far off, assisting the Contras."

"Am I supposed to defend the stupid CIA now?" I said, driving on. "Okay, I'm Hitler's daughter just by virtue of my passport. And you can feel just as smug as you want to, because you've struggled so hard to get yourself born a fucking Englishman."

"Thankfully," he said, "we've come to the waterfront and we can change the subject."

"If the CIA hadn't intervened in World War Two, you probably never would have been born."

"A little imprecise on dates and things," he said, "but I understand your point."

The hotel we were looking for was right on the bay, which was full of commerce and smelled like machinery. Because of the sight of Russians, maybe, I felt that everything on the blurry waters was secret and military—a big ship moving like a mystery across the view, and down to the south a huge docking area where it appeared a lot of construction was going on, lit with a fuzzy orange glow in the fog.

I felt how wonderful it would be to get out of here.

Although its sign had fallen down and been carted away somewhere, the hotel still showed the world a presentable face. The entrance gave onto a large barroom with an immensely high ceiling and bottles, many of them empty and plainly just for looks, behind the bar on shelves going up to the roof.

But the rest of the building, the part we were expected to sleep in, was like someone's basement; the floors were dirt, there were cobwebs . . . The walls were rough and armed with splinters, and actually these walls were nothing more than six-foot-high dividers serving to break up what was obviously, I realized, a *barn* into irregularly shaped stalls for humans. There was one electric light in a central spot way up in the rafters.

The owner wouldn't look at us. He was a youngish man—he'd travelled, probably, and knew he was bedding us down in a filthy swamp.

"Ah me. Oh boy," the Englishman said.

I felt sorrier for him than for myself.

"We'll be in Playas del Coco this time tomorrow. At a real resort," I promised.

In our stall were two cots covered by straw-filled mattresses. The owner lay clean sheets across the foot of the bed and disappeared.

Naturally we were the only patrons. Those with any sense slept in the street at a considerable savings and found equal comfort. But I exaggerate—the place had a freshwater shower in the smallest of the stalls surrounding us. I undressed while the Englishman went to stand under it, and then I stood under it with my eyes closed so as not to know about the bugs.

"Things are looking much, much brighter," he said when I got back to our part of the barn. "I have a pot of tea." He was just finishing a cup—actually it was not a cup, it was a glass. "I've got but the one cup," he said, and finishing it, he poured me some.

"And something else almost as wonderful," he said. He struck a ridiculous fencer's attitude: "I've bought an umbrella."

While I drank my tea, he commenced to reorganize his luggage.

In his own way he's a beautiful human, perhaps he's a hallucination, he's no easier to credit, in this obscene heat and dust, than a frail white snowflake. We're trying to outrun the Devil and everybody else, but for him it's that cozy minute before a journey when the tea tastes fine and the traveller isn't perturbed by the certain knowledge that all attempts at organization will fail. He's got his shirts right here, over there his trousers, got his little underthings all arranged, a pocket for the documents; he congratulates himself, silently but perceptibly, for his foresight—*two* notebooks, an umbrella—and you can see he feels no trepidation whatever at a moment when all others would, as I happen to, be carrying a cold weight in their hearts.

THERE WEREN'T any windows so it was hard to tell, exactly; but I judged it to be only a little past dawn when something woke me. Something, a certainty, a conviction . . .

"It's time for us to get out of here," I said, poking the Englishman over and over in his throat.

He rolled away, then turned over on his back and looked up at the ceiling without understanding it. "I was sleeping," he said.

"I'm sorry, but we'd better get out of here, I just know it."

"Why did you wake me?" he said as if he hadn't heard me.

"It's daylight. We've got to get a move on."

He turned toward me, lying on his arm, and saw me finally. "Where would we go? The border won't be open till—eight, did they say?"

"No, seven. We could sit in the car till they open it up."

"I can't think of anything more nerve-wracking. Do you forget I'm a hunted man?"

"I'm serious."

"Isn't this just how you felt the night before last?"

"This time I'm not kidding."

I started putting things in my purse. I was upset to say the least, grabbing useless things, a soiled Kleenex, an empty matchbox. "I'm leaving. And I'm taking the car."

"Don't be like this," he said.

"The best I can do for you is meet you later, at the bridge, where we let those soldiers off."

"Please."

"I'll meet you on the other side of the bridge."

"I'm staying with you," he said in absolute fear.

It was awful. He thought I'd abandon him. He didn't trust me, he had to guess, and second-guess, and guess again . . .

"Okay. Okay." I lay down on my cot, facing him.

In a few minutes I saw he was asleep again and I left. But I didn't get very far—he had the car keys in his pocket.

It was windy and grey outside. The owner was sweeping the wooden walk out front. There were several ships out on the harbor but none of them was taking me anywhere.

I asked the owner about breakfast.

They actually had my favorite, sopa negra. A poached egg floating in it justified my calling it breakfast. I ate at the bar.

It wasn't really a bar, it was a counter faced by wooden chairs.

There was no mirror back of it—just the shelves of bottles —or I'd have seen our redheaded American from Rivas come in behind me. As it was, he just turned up in the chair next to mine.

"You queer," I said by way of a greeting. To see him there absolutely ruined me. Now it was clear we were in a lot of trouble.

"I thought you'd be out of the country by now," he said.

"I'm not turning anybody in."

"I thought we'd made some sort of connection. I thought you understood . . . Okay, I was overly subtle. Let me be a little more direct. I'm asking you to help me with my report. Your British friend interests me, I'd like to include some background on him."

"Your report is all about him."

"More or less, yeah, you could say that. He gets a *lot* of ink, your friend does, because he's done a minor something that upsets the balance more knowledgeable people are trying to maintain from day to day down here, moment to moment, even—people who know more, people who *care* more than he does."

"I believe I'll sit by myself at the window." I moved my bowl and spoon to a table across the room.

I didn't eat much. The air held that tar-and-brine combo that made you feel already out at sea, and sick of it . . . Maybe this had been a resort once, but no more. Across the street was a very brief stretch of sand interrupted by blacktop boat-slips. Only two palm trees remained of the sunny era I'd anticipated entering here when the soldiers had said "resort," two trees sort of on the order of pachyderm feet, mashed into the sand . . .

I didn't leave, and neither did he. In another twenty minutes the fog had gone and the sunlight was burning up the dirt street. There'd been no rain for two days, I could feel it coming over the horizon though no sign of it was visible . . . The moment was suddenly narcotic, and although we were separated by half a room and the gulf of our pretenses, I think that fellow-feeling overcame each of us. Two Americans, two stupid Americans. Nobody will ever understand what that's like.

He rested his arm on the bar, the other hand in his pocket, his legs stretched out comfortably. And, finally, said something, talking across the room: "You know what I think? College never ends . . ."

I hated him for that, for starting in with his lies . . .

"Look at it this way," he said, getting up and coming over and joining me, "your travelling companion and I work for rival outfits. It's all this college-boy stuff, if you want to know the truth," he said. "Well, we'd like to fuck up their action. Basically, and it's really this simple, I need a signature on a report. And it has to be your signature."

"What are you sitting at my table for? Are you going to chase me all around the block? If you only knew how *sick* everybody gets looking at you, even knowing you exist. Don't you know what an *asshole* you are?"

"Don't you know what an asshole *he* is?" Now he leaned forward and took over the whole table . . . "He didn't just move things from one part of his desk to another part—he changed the future of two countries, do you see that? He turned over charts and documents and a whole economic *future* to an outlaw state."

I couldn't come back at him with anything but an empty, open mouth. The effect of this big talk was irresistible. The dream-like trouble chasing us took on force and a shape—charts, documents, the power of money.

"Whose side is your British friend on? In whose interest is he operating, or can you tell me in whose interest does he *think* he's operating?"

The infinite hopelessness of it left me floating: "I believe he said in the interest of fairness."

The pain that screwed up his face was genuine, I was convinced of that. "But the balances here, and the contests, are going according to *loyalties* to *people* and *groups*."

"Yeah."

"Yeah yeah *yeah*."

He put his hands behind his head and leaned back in his chair.

I said, "What if the oil's not there? Doesn't that blur the edges a little?"

"I'm a reporter. Aren't you a reporter? We make reports, don't we? What they do back at the main desk is beyond us. What goes on under the earth, as far as oil deposits and what-not, that's all out of my hands."

He leaned forward again. His expression was alert. A gust of wind blew a little dust and sea dampness through the doorway into the room; everything seemed to be waking up.

"But I'll tell you this," he said, "because I think the masks have fallen away, and you wouldn't be talking to me at this moment if you didn't think it was completely in your interest to be talking: What*ever* the situation as regards *oil*, at some point things are going to come down very hard on this man. If you insist on staying connected with him right up to that point, then at the very least it's going to hurt to feel that connection broken. Doesn't that make sense? And that's looking at it in the most positive light I possibly can. I'd be prepared for a bigger job coping on that day, frankly."

"You're so full of bullshit." I was embarrassed to sound like a child.

"Look, we're both in the business of reporting. Yesterday you were interested in me. Maybe you and I should pack in together after all."

"Pack in. Pack in? *Pack in?*"

"Okay. Okay," he said.

"You mean go with you? Are you threatening me with arrest?"

"You're so far off the mark," he said.

"Well what are you threatening me with, then?"

He rubbed his face. He looked at his watch. Perhaps he was wondering how much longer he had to go on being polite.

"Who would I be pulling for in this situation?" he asked. "Will you look around and tell me if you see any possible allies around here for me? Based on what I've been saying? I'm not threatening you. Everybody around here is threatening us. And especially you, because of your friend."

"What's wrong with my friend, really? What crime did he commit, really and truly?"

"I think somebody's going to have to take him out."

"*What?*"

"He's so completely off the map. Nobody knows what to do with him."

I was so stunned I couldn't think. "You lied. That's a threat," I said. "You said you weren't threatening," I cried out stupidly.

"Remember where we are," he said. "The connections down here are so sexy because down here this stuff really does happen. Isn't that why we all came down here?"

"Oh Down Here. Down Here . . . You said mistakes could be *corrected*."

I was weeping.

His attitude seemed to change completely. I didn't know what it was. It was as if he'd finished his drink, but actually he didn't have a drink. It was as if he were no longer thirsty.

"There," he said. "That's what I was talking about when I came up to you right here a few minutes ago."

He watched me a minute. "Are you listening to me?" he said.

I nodded.

"You cross the border this afternoon. You go to Liberia, and you get a bus to Los Chiles."

"Los Chiles? Where on earth is that?"

"It's a few dozen miles northeast of Liberia, right on the San Juan river. Border town."

"What do we want to do there?"

"Assuming everything's gone off okay, that's where you get paid."

He didn't understand anything—life! words! faces! moments!

He'd made me cry, he'd scared me, he'd beaten me at the game of conversation. But he hadn't *won* . . .

"There's nothing to get paid for. I'm not signing anything."

"You'll sign when you get a halfway grown-up understanding of the goddamn *situation*. Which is going to be soon."

"Go to hell."

He got up from the table, and my first thought was that I'd driven him off with curses.

But actually he was rising, with a bright smile, to greet the Englishman: "I just got into town."

"How remarkable to see you again. Especially here," he said.

"I know, it's weird, it's great," the American agreed, "I'm really glad. What are you guys doing? Should we pal around a little this afternoon? See the sights?"

The Englishman ignored all that. "The manager fellow is brewing me some tea," he told me. "I'll be in the room, is that all right? We should be thinking about an early start."

"Okay," I said.

Maybe he saw that I'd been crying, because he asked, "Are you all right?"

"I'm okay," I said. "I'm going with you."

"We'll talk again, okay?" the American said.

The Englishman looked at him, and then at me. By straining to cover up his anger, he made his face seem young and weak. "I don't have anything to say to you," he told the consultant.

"I wasn't suggesting you did," the American said as I stood up. "But maybe others do."

I looked around for someone to bring me the check, but the three of us were alone in the place. The Englishman was already leaving, and I followed him feeling defensive and ashamed.

We went back to the room, where I poured the tea into our single glass as the Englishman stood beside his suitcase opening and closing his umbrella with a succession of breezy whooshes.

"It rains quite a bit in Costa Rica, doesn't it?"

"It rains a hell of a lot in Nicaragua, too, didn't you notice?"

"I'm very glad," he said, "to have an umbrella."

But I could tell he wanted to know what we'd talked about. He was just too afraid, or too polite, to ask. I could tell he'd reached a point of tightly bound panic because he couldn't trust anyone, least of all me.

But in a minute he started in: "Onward and upward," he said. "I hope we have enough petrol to reach the border. I thought you said we had a half a tank, was it half a tank," he said, "do we have enough gasoline? I'm afraid I really don't care whether we have enough, by God I'll walk as far as necessary to get out of here. I think we should try for the northern border," he said suddenly, "I'm not sure about Costa Rica at all . . . I don't think we should fool around with the Costa Rican border, we've drawn too much notice. It may be we've—telegraphed our intentions . . . What are you looking at? Isn't it obvious?—we never should have come here. We've done everything wrong. But it's not too late to change our plans . . .

"What would you say," he pestered me, "is there anything you can add to this? Anything at all you can add?"

He looked at me like a beggar, waiting for me to confess whatever I might have done.

But I didn't know what I'd done. I honestly didn't know. I thought I'd held out, given nothing away . . . "Will you relax? We just talked about exchanging cordobas over the border."

He wasn't satisfied with that. But again good breeding checked him from interrogating me.

He sat down on his cot and seemed to be testing the tensile strength of his new umbrella, resting his hands on it like a cane.

"Maybe we should sneak around the checkpoints somehow," I said.

"Sneak."

"Is there something wrong with your hearing? I mean smuggle ourselves across the border."

"No," he said without a second's reflection, "I wouldn't want to try anything like that."

He of the weightless, invisible cojones!

"Oh, for Christ's sake," I said, "it can't be that hard to cross illegally. The Contras are all the time wandering in and out of here, you know." I was getting a little testy, granted; however, his blatantly spineless attitude was taxing my civility.

And apparently something was taxing his: "Will you please shut up? And let's simply turn our minds to the legal options?"

"Oh do let's."

"We can—turn around, give ourselves up to the American Embassy or the British Consul."

"Yes. Right. We can do the Embassy."

"Or, as I say, we could go north to Honduras."

"We could do Honduras."

"And as one leftist nation to another we might cross more easily into El Salvador."

"Yeah. Yeah. We could do El Sal. Only there's no common border with El Sal."

He got up, trembling.

"You are a North American female prostitute-drifter with a press card," he said, "which has been revoked. You drink like an Apache. You'll end by killing us both. So much is obvious about you that you really ought to just," but he ended stammering, "just—shut up."

His face had turned white, and I thought the tears would flow.

But all I needed was some upper-crust lightweight giving me hallelujah about my circumstances. "Don't forget, honey," I said, "the night you found me you were looking for a whore."

That got him marching around the room aimlessly. He seemed to cast back through the events comprising his life, and then his defeated face agreed that, yes, he had been looking for just that kind of person, and so he sat down and kept quiet for a change.

"Sorry." I don't know why I said it, I wasn't sorry at all . . .

"Look here now," he said, "leave the money behind, will you? And I'll be certain to redeem it when I can get some dollars, if you can't afford to lose it—just, please, don't risk our plans."

"I can make a decent exchange at the border. I won't lose my ass."

"I'll give you a better price than he"—he reconsidered his terminology—"a better rate, whatever your arrangement—"

"What do you mean, whatever my arrangement? You were right there. You know the arrangement."

"Oh, God, all this, having my tit caught in a wringer—my ass in a sling." I couldn't tell if he was sweating or spilling tears down his cheeks. Pretty soon we were laughing together. There's nothing like hysteria, and thunder in the clouds, to convince you nothing matters.

"It's just that he can't be trusted. Of course you see that."

"He can be trusted to sell us out," I said.

"No. Nothing is certain, not even that."

"Look, everybody sells everybody out down here. They can't afford not to, it's basic, that's the situation. If you hang on to even one little tiny scruple it'll be the death of you, I promise. This is Hell, it's Hell, how many times do you have to be told?"

"This is apropos of nothing. Are you talking to me or to yourself? You seem to be suggesting that I be the one to throw somebody to the wolves, but I see nobody in the vicinity to be thrown. Do you?"

I was caught up in a cloud of rage . . . I sensed cool sanity drifting just beneath me but I couldn't reach it. "All I'm saying is be ready. Be ready to find out that this is Hell."

"It isn't Hell. This is all *quite* real."

"If it wasn't real, it wouldn't be Hell."

That seemed to get him thinking.

"You do have a vivid world view," he said.

THE ENGLISHMAN didn't like driving on the right. But he drove us to the border anyway. He needed to dominate something, if only a steering wheel.

He'd used up all his words for the time being. Even after we'd crept up the dirt streets and gotten past all of the stores and houses we'd seen last night and crossed the bridge out of town—it stood empty of sentries in the daylight—he kept quiet.

I watched the last of Nicaragua go by. We passed along a stretch of Panamerican Highway quite typical of the south, running a sparse gantlet of crippled vehicles—and here and there a dead dog stretched out beside the road, and wrecked, flip-flopping chickens, and your occasional truck-struck horse, still somewhat alive in the dirt, hindquarters jerking and the all-too-visible ribcage heaving with the desire to get back up and go on protractedly starving . . .

We came into the tunnel of tall grasses we'd gone through last night. I wondered if the same soldiers would be at the crossing now . . . Whereas I should have felt the terror searching between my ribs for my heart, what I actually remember experiencing was self-consciousness and embarrassment. Instead of a fluttery vertigo I felt a speechless irritation, a paralyzing disgust for every insect that killed itself on the window, a defeated feeling that I was through with sugar fields, a heavy, sleepy hatred for the Englishman that actually made me slur my words when I talked to him . . . And then I wanted to make love with him, I wanted to taste his skin . . . I realized that I hated my hands, and that my clothes wouldn't stop touching me . . .

Anger is fear. Lust is fear. Grief, excitement, weariness are fear—just feel down far enough, look hard enough.

My words came out small and whining: "Oh God, oh God, I hope nothing happens . . ."

I told him I wanted to see everything destroyed before I had to look at any more of it.

He didn't talk at all.

And the Englishman kept his thoughts to himself even after we were stopped ten miles down the highway with the walls of grass growing on either side of us, in the line of cars waiting to get out of this horrible land.

Someday the Marines would come down from the sky and strafe this convoy of hopefuls. Would come in a plague of U.S. gunships like big lightbulbs in the nighttime, sowing down on them all a lot of Dow chemicals, drifting and winking leaflets full of unintelligible threats and bribes, and high-caliber Gatling tracer-bullets . . . And giant firebombs . . .

We spent a good hour moving down the last mile of Nicaraguan roadway full of holes, turning the engine off and letting it rest between our yards-long advances toward that first kiosk.

Behind us in the line was a group of boys with a huge transistor radio, all four of them wearing the kind of sunglasses I associate with French film stars, in a tall convertible jeep with Panamanian plates. Their jeans were impossibly blue, their tee-shirts white as glaciers . . .

On the other hand, ahead of us was one of those buses that

seem to drift out of history from Buchenwald and turn up in the Third World to take impoverished people home. The passengers had all gotten out and were wandering up and down beside this strange craft looking patient and content.

We stayed in the car—out of an unspoken mutual terror of exposing our faces, I'm sure. And still the Englishman hadn't said one word since San Juan del Sur—two hours ago.

He kept quiet as we got past the first checkpoint, where last night the cable stretched across the road had stopped us. Our documents were fine; nobody bothered about us at all. Up ahead, it appeared, we would have to get out and complete some forms, and then wait while our car was searched.

It was phenomenal: a few hundred yards down the road was Costa Rica, and I swear to you that on that side of the verge the palm trees were taller, the fields a more subtle shade of green, and the highway moved up into cool mountains without a bump or a hole in its pavement. And everyone was better dressed, and there weren't so many bugs.

The sun came over the easternmost of those mountains all too soon. The windshield grew hot to the touch. Eerie shafts of light, reflecting from the glass parts of jeeps and trucks, flew up through the dust-cloud ahead.

A shadow passed over us trailing a vague, light rain; and in two minutes the day was bright again.

"We'll pass out if we stay in this car," I said.

The Englishman didn't answer me.

"You haven't said a word in almost—a long time," I said. "You're thinking too hard. Don't do that, not in this heat, okay?"

Later I said, "The temperature is fatal." I was drenched; but there was something narcotic about simply giving in, letting myself be cooked. The line of cars moved slowly, to say the least. The Panamanian boppers behind us had taken to the shade by the road and fallen asleep on the grass. "I didn't think so many people would be here so early. Look at all the *people*."

I couldn't help saying such things, the Englishman's cold treatment was making me nervous.

But for once he answered me. "Maybe this is better, all this crowding, as they'll have less time to . . ." He didn't go so far as to name the possibility.

T H E R E ' S N O conveying the state we'd reached. Let it be enough to say that as we'd sat in the car and stood by the car, we'd seen most of the people around us walking over to the second kiosk to surrender their Nicaraguan travel papers. We wouldn't be able to go any farther until we did the same. But we behaved, the both of us, as if we were certain that something *else* had to happen first, maybe that an official had to approach, look at our papers, and pass us along, or the car in front of us had to disappear—exactly what trick my fear-struck mind was playing I can't remember . . . The point is that the next move in getting on toward Costa Rica was ours, that was the procedure here, but we did nothing. We did nothing for hours. Such was the obliterating strength of our fate.

Basically this border station was a little settlement occurring between two roadblocks—stores, residences, a barracks, some offices, everything made of soggy lumber, like a jungle village. Across the highway was a chapel with its doors and windows boarded over.

In the afternoon I went behind the church to pee—this was the only private place I'd found to do it the day I'd come into this country. Now I watered the same patch of grass again . . . Everything was still happening twice . . . As I was done, I had a picture of myself running away into the field and shrinking out of sight.

When I got back to the car, he wasn't there. Everything was in motion suddenly. The locks on his heart were shattered, and he was standing in the line at the second kiosk with his papers in his hand. He was just like the rest of them in the line: unhurried, bedraggled, lobotomized.

He watched me as we gave them our passports and papers.

"I pray to God you got rid of that money back there," the Englishman said.

I couldn't say anything. I hadn't.

The money? . . . I hadn't even thought about it.

He couldn't say anything either. But he was so excruciated that if I'd touched him with a hand, my hand would have hurt, I know it.

But now I understood what he'd been waiting for—what he'd put off saying. Why he hadn't gone up to the kiosk until now. He'd asked me once, and he was too civilized to go on demanding that I not endanger us. Now, it seemed to him, I'd had a chance to do the right thing . . .

I put him straight. "The limit is only for currency you bring in. They don't care how much you take *out*—they're glad to see their stupid currency go."

"But you mean to say you didn't put it away back there? Out back of the church?"

"No."

"But I was sure you had."

"I told you, they're glad to see it carted out of their miserable country. It's worthless. Here," I said, losing my grip altogether suddenly and going after the money in my purse, "here, do you need some toilet paper?"

"But you're over the limit by *thousands*—*tens* of thousands. It's just too irregular, you'll call attention to us . . ."

"Oh, big fucking deal," I said, just to be talking back.

"It's fine of you to want to destroy everything between us, but do you have to be so unbearably stupid about it?"

"Oh—stewpid," I said. "Stewpid."

Okay, okay. But he'd shocked me by laying his finger so deftly on—was it the truth, was I doing something irrevocable and crazy just to break us up? I didn't know. It was hot, I couldn't breathe, I couldn't think.

But the suggestion drove me to produce nonsense. "Answer me, do you need some toilet paper or not? When *do* you shit, anyway? I've never seen you," and so on.

"This is so silly," the Englishman said, "*I'm* silly, I've been an absolute *fool*. You're a sick woman, you're very ill . . ."

And he continued, now addressing the young civilian approaching us for the search: "And she would *have* to be disturbed, you see—a woman peddling herself in the cocktail bars, without any reason for doing it, so much to recommend her—take pity on this woman, she's ill—loco, loco . . .

"I'm being sacrificed," he said to me. "You're destroying me." And he announced: "It probably has to do with your father."

Oh, you smug patrician lisping asshole shit . . .

"Don't think because we rolled around a couple times and got sweaty, now I'm ready to start laying out the life story of my father and how I got to be a whore," I said, "hey, what are you all of a sudden, a therapist?" He really wanted to talk about my father! "If I feel like a catharsis, I can just step out in the road and take an AK-47 in the ear. Can't I."

Not that he was carefully following all this . . . No, he was watching the customs officer.

And he didn't have to watch very long—the man found the money right away. It was there in my purse, an old white envelope wilted around a brick of cordobas.

"There," the Englishman said. He resigned; he sank down behind his eyes and shut up.

I tried to smile at the young man weighing my money in his hand. "I'm going away. I'm crossing the border. It's nothing," I insisted. "No problem."

"Where did you get this Nicaraguan currency?" his superior, a man also in civil dress, asked when he was brought over.

"No problem," I said.

He laughed, repeating this phrase as he took a pen from behind his ear and filled out a receipt for me. "How much?" he said, beginning to count the money.

I had to shrug. "Don't know."

"No problem, no problem," he said to the younger one. He whistled ostentatiously and rolled his eyes at the final count, which he said out loud, but large numbers in Spanish go right by me . . . He took the money back to the office, leaving us with the younger man and also the receipt, on which he'd written a figure close to sixty thousand.

The assistant, as if he hadn't already seen the money, sidled around and looked at this number, duplicating his boss's admiring whistle.

SPEAKING ENGLISH, the customs officer directed the Englishman to a chair outside. "Sit down," he beamed, "there's going to be some delay now." His glee was not masked. "*Come* in, *come* in," he said to me.

As he questioned me he pursed his lips and tried to look stern, but his eyes shone. I was not a bore, that was it. His job was a bore; this was not.

I held on to the sides of my wooden chair, before his desk,

faking nonchalance and answering his questions truthfully. Why bother lying now? We established that I'd arrived here from Costa Rica four months ago.

"Where are you going?"

"Back to Costa Rica. And then to the U.S."

"You have some friends in Costa Rica? Some Nicaraguan friends who sell you money? These people we call them Contras?"

He clasped his hands in front of him on the desk, and leaned forward over them pleasantly. "How much have you paid for these cordobas?"

"I don't remember, exactly," I began, but he interrupted me by going into a rage and slapping his hand on his desk several times—

"Fuck yourself you don't remember! That's a lot of bullshit!"

"Wait, please don't be angry—I mean I don't remember *exactly*, but around two hundred ten cordobas to the dollar."

"There. It's much better."

"I'm cooperating with you completely," I said in Spanish.

"Forgive me for forgetting that I'm a gentleman and you are a lady," he said, also in Spanish.

This surprised me almost to the point of tears.

In English he said brightly, "All right, my dear! I have your passports, and I must make one phone call or two. It's necessary."

"Please," he said when we'd rejoined the desolate Englishman, "get some drink, enjoy your lunch, here is my associate, he will be your guide, is it okay? There's going to be a delay, I made it clear already."

His associate, the younger man who'd called all this nuisance down on us, smiled sheepishly, I believed, and pointed out a kiosk that sold food.

"Are you hungry?" I said, not looking too directly at the Englishman.

"No," he told me.

W I T H I N A N hour the car had been officially impounded and our passports confiscated. We were taken to a military encampment several miles east of the Panamerican Highway to await civil arrest.

The truck we rode in the back of broke down before we reached the end of the jungle path. Under the not-too-watchful custody of our guard of three soldiers we got out and walked, our shoes slipping on a pabulum of melted leaves. Again I was granted an awareness that my sensations—the thirst, irritation, anger, also unexpected attacks of peace and benevolence—were only the forms of fear, the thousand faces of adrenaline . . . It was still afternoon but there would be a Night Person back in here somewhere to receive us, no doubt, a tormentor or henchling, there will always be a Night Person.

In no time I was ready to vomit, having conjured for myself a vague spider-shadow toward which we floated . . .

Fear blocked my sight—made irrelevant whatever was immediately around—in effect, drained the normally clotted jungle of visible things, and I was deaf, too, to anything but an inner pleading, What do I do now, how do I cope, this can't be as bad as it seems, but if it's as bad as it seems, what do I do now, how do I cope? . . . But then all of a sudden I surfaced momentarily and several yards of scenery produced themselves like a photograph. I was stunned by what I saw. This jungle road, two ruts through a musky vegetable dimness, all of this, branches and bouquets and the shocks of leaves—even sounds, even the chirping of birds—was steeped in humidity like bandages in one of those foreign soporifics such as reserpine . . . Every few heartbeats a bird floated up across the path far ahead of us. The sunlight lay like money on the jungle floor, and here and there, where the roof of trees was ripped, it came down in a torrent, in other places it fell in shafts as thin as a glassblower's rod . . . We reached the encampment, and there was the Army of Nicaragua—as usual a lot of pestiferous urchins dirty as pigs . . .

Out of nervousness, the couple of dozen soldiers in the clearing pretended not to see us. They posed for us in their sea-green utilities, the highlights on their rifles quivering like shards of porcelain, as if they always gripped their weapons like this and sat around all day without moving or uttering words. Before the blizzard of fear-blindness swallowed me again I formed an impression of squalor from just a few things, from the smashed watermelons, the lukewarm bottles of strawberry pop, the rain of bugs off Lago de Nicaragua.

They put us in their headquarters, a cinderblock building about half a story high—the corrugated roof had been laid over it prematurely, it appeared, to provide a minimal shelter while more cinderblock found its way here from the North Pole . . . Waiting to be completed, that's the motif . . . Elaborations of it will fill every page of the history of this revolution . . .

We couldn't quite stand upright inside it. I might have complained, but some of the soldiers had sacrificed this, their living space, for the two of us.

And all complaints and all conversations were forestalled by the endless shrieking of what I at first took to be heavy machinery in the dale out back—screaming girders pulverized by giant grindstones . . .

It was the locals slaughtering hogs or whatever—hacking them with axes or beating them to death with sledges, I didn't know, our open doorway and half-sized windows faced the other direction—anyway they were providing themselves with meat.

And all afternoon I was thinking, with shame and embarrassment, about what would happen to me when I had to go to the bathroom. The question was as large in my mind as all the rest of it, all this being arrested and taken out into the jungle and possibly, for all I knew, being shot and buried.

The slaughtering must have been a seasonal endeavor, because every pig in the land seemed to be getting it . . . They kept up squealing all afternoon and didn't stop until suppertime. You just wouldn't think any living thing would have that much breath in its body.

Right through the doorway we could see the soldiers' kiosk, country women combing through a wicker tray of rice for pebbles or sticks, and monster pots brewing up something steamy. But I wasn't feeling hungry just yet.

"I've made a terrible mistake of everything," the Englishman said.

I'd been thinking the same thing about myself.

He said, "There are spiritual principles at work here."

"My. Aren't you swift to grasp?"

"Your attitudinizing really doesn't protect you, you know, not from anything important."

"Does it protect me from dinner? What about dinner?"

"That's up to them, I would presume."

"Maybe we have to make a noise about it before they decide to feed us."

But we didn't say anything. He sat beside me, in my corner there.

He wanted to take me in his arms. "No, it's too hot." I let him hold me for a while nevertheless.

I felt sweaty, sticky—I felt slimy. This is one of those things it's difficult to put into words: yet letting him hold me I felt more like a whore than I did being lowered down upon by a naked stranger and thinking only about the money.

"I'm sorry I was such a bear," he said.

That was funny to me—"I do like the way you talk," I said.

"I know we've been under equal stress. We'll have to give each other the benefit of the doubt, does that sound reasonable? Listen, can you talk to these people? You know the language, you were with soldiers up in Matagalpa, wasn't it, you—helped them. I'm in your hands, I'm afraid."

Oh, poor man, in *my* hands . . .

I said, "I was only up north a couple months. Actually it was one month. I was late with my first report, I kept putting it off . . . When the second one was already due and I still hadn't done the first one—*I* don't know. I left! Actually I'd made up my mind before that. I was gone from the first day."

"My God, we're so much alike . . ."

It made me uncomfortable to hear somebody say this. Anybody at all.

"One attempt, one gesture," he said. "Something to bring you back . . . It comes up empty . . . You go on as always. As always . . . And then that one thing, that one attempt becomes a sort of ugly lump, doesn't it. Almost a cancer. That act that was supposed to be good. The thing that was going to bring you back, it becomes an obscenity."

I knew what he was talking about. I knew exactly. "That's a boring theory," I told him.

He was strong. He just asked the guard, who was some distance away paying more attention to the women than to us, for some food and water. The guard mocked his gestures, laughing, and said he'd find out if it was permitted.

THAT NIGHT, an explosion of thunder and water drew me slowly out of sleep. Flashlights herded us out into the middle of the night, through the rain, into a church on the other side of the dale. Not that we prisoners were in any hazard of a soaking until they got us wet—not under our corrugated roof. But the soldiers had all been sleeping in hammocks, and the bits of plastic sheet they depended on probably didn't work against such a downpour.

The church's floors felt cool when we lay down on them —they were stone, or tile, I couldn't tell by the small glow of votive candles in the corners. The candles were far off, it was a sizeable church, the town must have been populous—certainly there'd been a fair number of barnyard animals going under the knife that afternoon—exactly as up north, you thought you'd lost contact forever, but it turned out a small civilization thrived just over the next shrub.

It was true. The next morning we found that the church square opened into a tiny town of a few buildings whose purposes remained unexplained. Nobody was out on the streets except soldiers.

The air was cool and wet. After our breakfast of rice and beans they let the Englishman relax in the doorway, in a patch of sun next to the tub of holy water.

But me they took into town to see a full-Tenente at a Sandinista campaign office, which also apparently served as the area's military headquarters.

I was looked after first, silently, by a frightening person who came from the back and took charge of me with the slowness of somebody just awakened from a coma, an older enlisted man in a clean white undershirt and mud-encrusted combat boots.

In Managua almost every soldier I'd met had seemed just another citizen of the general stupefaction; but these people, hardened by this rural life and very often by actual combat, were of quite another order. "Good day," I said to him as he searched me. "Are you ordered to search me, or do you like to touch me?" He had no right to be feeling my ass . . .

He didn't answer, but he looked hard at me. Actually, I saw nothing of his face except for two eyes brilliant with fatigue and irritation, but I created for him one of those interrogator-faces from films and television, a cruel, deceptive face, at first bland and dreamy, suggesting interstellar distances, and turning suddenly into a cage for his inward, rabid self.

This man took me into the rear office and stood by the window while I talked with the Tenente.

The Tenente sat behind his desk, comfortably, with one leg crossed over the other, examining papers prefatory to our interview. I knew these papers had nothing to do with his thoughts. What made him think it was necessary to pretend like that?

On the wall behind the desk was a poster invoking Efficiency & Discipline, a sentiment I found too ridiculous, considering the nation around us, even to be a joke—riveting, in fact, for its psychopathic denial of all experience . . . Beside it was a poster presenting the photograph of an old woman in the embrace of someone who looked a lot like Daniel Ortega. And the caption read in Spanish:

Mother,
where they speak your name
it says victory . . .

They don't ask much of life, these revolutionaries. To sit at the desk there with the telephone in the flickering light and know that the grown-ups are never coming back: this is the peace of man . . .

I sat before the Tenente quietly, but inside I was covering up my head with my hands . . . Reasons, images, memories came at me, the advance weapons of fear. I drove myself out into the street and whipped her, pleaded forgiveness from the dust as I was whipped . . . Just because I'd wanted to help the Englishman . . . While forgetting to stay objective I'd leaned my elbow inadvertently on the Fate lever. I'd brought it all down on my own head.

The Tenente's lollygagging had its desired effect. I weakened myself considerably while nothing happened at all.

In his own language he said, "Why do you come to this country and make yourself to be such a nuisance?"

Get to the point! Will I live?

But I could only shake my head and say: "I'm sorry."

He was different. It was the way he looked at me. It had something to do with the chemistry he generated, or rather didn't generate . . . For him there was no more of the swooping between grandiosity and resignation that usually characterized the demeanor, from moment to moment, of the Latin men I knew. Whatever powered those flights had been leached out of him.

"Your passport."

"Certainly, I carry my name and my face right here, I keep them hidden between my tits . . ."

"Please speak Spanish. It's true you speak it?"

"The other man took my passport and the Englishman's passport also."

"Who took them?"

"The customs officer."

"Ah. It's clear," he said.

"Good."

I might have been applying for a job I didn't really want, a job they didn't really have available . . . We might have been stewing in a void of casual and absurd lies like that . . .

Why didn't he scream at me, why didn't he accuse me, force out of me a gang of crippled reasons for the fact that I was down here watching what my government was doing to their homeland?

What was the matter? Didn't he like me?

I began to get the idea that his whole purpose in having me here was to confiscate my passport; and now, having failed, he didn't know what to do with me without looking like a fool.

"How do you expect to profit from dealing in our currency?"

"I'm sorry. I'm very, very sorry. I didn't expect to profit."

"Why did you come to Nicaragua?"

Through the window I saw the red-haired American walking past in the dirt street.

I heard a car or jeep start up outside, drive a short way, and stop with its engine off.

I told the Tenente: "I came here to see the Devil with my eyes."

The Tenente and the other one stood together watching out the window a minute while he talked low. I made out the one word ". . . político . . ."

He came back and looked at me with his face cooking.

"Crazy," he said.

OH I HAD a lot of bold thoughts, waiting in there for him. I recited the lines of William Something Merwin:

I will not bow in the middle of the room
To the statue of nothing
With the flies turning around it.

But the last line of the verse seemed to belong, when he entered, to the redhead:

On these four walls I am the writing.

"I'm cooperating here," I said with the confused love of a child for its father when its father is enraged.

But he didn't answer me.

I said, "I had a feeling about you."

As far as he was concerned, supposedly, I wasn't present. He took a minute to look around the room as if he'd come about renting it. Then as soon as he "noticed" me he started right in:

"Look, you're U.S., I'm U.S., I'd like to treat you with respect. But I'm sure you yourself would have to admit, you've been all over the place lately. As far as being a representative of your country, you get very poor marks. You've lost your rights, and you're in more fucking trouble than you can handle. Do you cut him loose or do you eat whatever they're going to make him eat?"

"Who do you mean? The Sandinistas? He was *helping* them."

"We're in the process of turning that information around."

I was beaten, completely beaten, or I might have asked him who in the world he *was* and what he *meant*. But as it rested I was not well, and what I didn't understand I ignored.

"Are you a journalist or not?" he said. "This is the story of a lifetime, wandering around with a hunted British oil executive—and this is the leverage where I get *you* out of this; you're a dumb señorita, excuse me, but that goes a *long* way

with these folks, you're a journalist with a respected magazine
—you choose the magazine, I'll get a telex down here for you
within twenty-four hours—and you were by *no means* his
accomplice—as of right now you cut him loose, you dump
his act—"

"I cut his *throat* you mean, I stab his *back*—"

He wasn't liking his work. He threw me a look like that of
someone being burned at the stake. I fancy he didn't guess
how naked he was.

I was every bit as naked . . . He saw me. There wasn't anywhere on Earth he wouldn't be looking right at me and seeing
my breasts, the veins in my belly, the curling hair over my
vagina. I felt intensely embarrassed, I felt like exploding, I
felt like crying, and then I was crying at last, I was weeping,
weeping—

What a relief, like coming home—

"Oh, hey," he said when he saw my tears, "I *get* that all
this wasn't in the plan." He summoned up some sort of air of
professionalism. "This is a rough one. But either you do it and
get out of the way, or you let it happen to him right on
top of you. You have *fucked up*. Remember I said before
that mistakes can be corrected? Well this is a big mistake.
Maybe to put this one behind you you'll have to reach right
down into your guts and tear them out. It's not possible for
you to do anything else. It's all you can do. You have no
choice."

"No choice."

"You have no choice."

"It's 1984."

"Yeah," he said, "that's right, you could say that."

How good it felt! To be sitting down in the dirt and giving
up.

He began bargaining over the blame with me: "Half the
trouble here is my fault, I admit that," he said, "just let me

do what I can, okay? Let me make up for it. I'm just looking for some way of getting you across the border."

"If I sign, you'll get me out of this place?"

"That's all it takes, I believe. To be honest, a lot of this is out of my hands. But I feel sure enough to make it a quid pro quo—getting you across that border."

"Me, you're saying. Just me."

"What do you mean? No," he said, "both of you."

DID THIS conversation really happen? Or is it just the same conversation I'm always having here in Hell? Does Hell consist merely of that one conversation leading to the date, 1984—the recognition of my absolute imprisonment, the ineluctability of my everything—does my life consist of that single dialog sketched out and framed in an infinite variety of situations?

The act of signing—how is that proved? I don't remember signing my name. To this day I wonder if I actually signed my name.

Wouldn't there be some record of a move like that, luminous singing *scars* where my fingers touched the pen?

But I know that down here you have to deal. That's the mystery of the reality of down here. That's why I descended into this place, and now was the fated moment.

"I'm not free."

"That's right," he said, "that's right, that's right."

How good it felt!

THAT AFTERNOON when I got back to the church, the Englishman was still there. It was hot again, really oppressive. I wanted a drink of rum with ice, but I didn't bother asking for one. Outside the plantain and arbolitos looked bedraggled after the night's hard rain. The soldiers must have decided it wasn't going to storm anymore, because they began gathering their equipment together.

They marched us out the door and alongside the church, back the same way we'd come in the dark and the rain last night, and I was shocked—more than shocked; I thought I'd known whatever there was to know of disorientation and miserable wonder by now, but this was beyond all—to see, around the corner of the church, several large shrubs cut into shapes: an elephant, a dog, two swans putting out their long necks toward each other in a green leafy kiss. I'd never seen a topiary garden before, had never expected to see one, couldn't even have explained why I should know the English term for this collection of organic statues. What a silly world. A brief flagstone path wound among these four shapes in a side yard not half the size of a tennis court.

"Did you see that?" I asked the Englishman after we'd gone into the dale and were heading up the side of it toward the encampment.

"See what?" he said.

"A topiary garden." He turned to look back at me and down the line of soldiers to the bottom of the dell. The men ahead of him paid no mind and kept right on trudging upward—we might have lit out into the jungle at that moment, if we'd only known which way to run. "A garden, no. I'm sorry to say I missed it altogether," he said.

Before they put us back in our child-size cinderblock, they took us to bathe ourselves at the well. Honestly, it was just a mud-hole sleeping in a jail of sunbeams at the end of a path. We took turns dipping a wooden bowl down into it, as we balanced on the well's tiny embankment of muck, and pouring the water over our heads.

In no time at all the well was muddy-looking. I prayed about snakes, and worried I might slip down into the hole and wondered just how deep it went. But the cool water was like heroin.

"Oh!" the Englishman cried, "that's good, that's wonderful." He didn't say anything else.

BY THAT night he couldn't hide his feelings. He was in a frenzy to ask me what was going on. I couldn't see his face because they wouldn't give us a light, yet I felt his tension in the way he sat against the wall, with his neck stiff and his head held up. Still he was silent for a while in that restraint of his, in that simple unfounded and useless decency that would kill him soon.

His suspicions got hold of him completely finally. "I wonder why they aren't talking to me? Why are they only talking to you? Why are they talking to you at all," he pleaded, "what have you got to tell them?"

I couldn't shut him up. "We've only been here a day. It'll be your turn soon. They'll probably talk to you tomorrow."

"But what did you find to talk to them about?"

"Nothing!"

"Then why did they keep you all afternoon?"

"Oh, I see. Do you want logic? That isn't Scotland Yard out there, it's practically the middle of the equator. Everybody's brains are fried. Everybody's stupid."

"Don't evade me. It's essential you be *candid*. Please. Don't leave me in the dark."

"Look, I'm not functioning," I said, "I told them I know they're demons and I said I wanted to see Satan himself, I'm not functioning!"

"Are you serious? Do you mean to say you carried your little metaphor into your communications with these people?"

"I told them I don't love you!"

"It's all right," he said, "I'm sorry I asked, you're right. Of course it's your affair and none of mine."

"They told me this is Hell, and I can't love you."

"I apologize," he said, "I was wrong to pry."

"There's a war on. And war is Hell. That's not a metaphor. That's what war is. That's what Hell is."

At this point he took off his shirt and draped it over the windowsill to take the air.

I'll never be told whether through all this he was held in check by great discipline, or only paralyzed. Nobody will ever be able to tell me.

"I signed something."

"Oh," was the best he could do. Then, "You signed something."

Then he said: "What was it, exactly, that you signed?"

"I don't know. I didn't ask. Does it matter?"

"Yes. It does."

"Well, not to me."

"It's all right," he said defiantly. "All of this can be worked out somehow. The important thing is that I'm with you because I love you."

If he was playing games it was disgusting—and if he meant it, it was disgusting anyway, that he chose this moment to say it.

I had to remind him: "Just don't forget what you were looking for when you found me."

"I won't forget," he said, "how can I forget?"

Speechlessly he put his head in his hands.

Then he started in torturing me with his explanations, which were exactly like my own explanations.

"I think I began by . . . Well, I suppose I was curious. I started out feeling that I wanted to know you, I had to watch you in action, observe you, you understand."

"Oh no, wait . . ."

"But I ended by feeling that you needed my help . . ."

"Stop, wait, stop. Are you talking? Or am I?"

What he's doing is what I'm doing; what I thought he was—is what I am—

Just as when we were loving, honeymooning . . . There was only one of us . . .

But if there is only one of us, then I'm alone.

TWO MEN from the Costa Rican Guardia picked us up in an aluminum boat after sunset, when the bugs had reached the peak of their feeding-frenzy. "Horrible," the Englishman said. These insects were like bullets whining in the air. They got in your orifices.

"Are you the Rural or the Civil Guard?" I asked, getting into the boat.

"We are the Rural," one of them said, and identified himself as a captain.

"Ay! Ay!" the other said, meaning the bugs.

We passed slowly along across the San Juan, a sleepy river overgrown with the images of stars. The Río San Juan feeds into Lago de Nicaragua, the only freshwater lake in the world to have sharks. The sharks come up a channel from the Atlantic and find the lake. I didn't think they would ever get into the San Juan, but it was something to consider before taking a swim . . .

The motor was small and hummed absentmindedly, almost like an insect itself.

On the Nicaragua side of the Río San Juan there was nothing but jungle. Across the river, in Costa Rican territory, a pier began, going back over marsh and mush toward dry land. On this pier a sentry walked. When the engine stopped we could hear him clicking the safety of his rifle on and off nervously.

And then at the end of the pier, where Costa Rica began, there was the oddest thing, a large deck with a bar, all lit up. On the bar a television sat in a cloud of moths, and the bartender was simply waiting all alone behind it, surrounded by a void.

There couldn't possibly have been any customers for him in this wilderness, other than the sentry making a regular series of noises in the darkness at the other end of the pier. And now the four of us.

The bartender served up a gin and tonic for me, and a Coke for the Englishman. He was watching a Spanish-dubbed version of *The Gang That Couldn't Shoot Straight*.

"Thank you," I told the two Guardia. "Will you drink with us?"

"Not now."

The enlisted man bit his lip hearing this. But the Captain was in charge of the whole outfit, and he wanted to show us how irritated he was at having been sent out at night.

"Your loss," I said.

"Please," the Englishman said. I didn't know if he was talking to me or the Captain.

"Okay, I'll practice my English with you," the Captain said, and the enlisted man smiled happily.

They had a beer with us and loosened their shirts. The Captain identified his weapon as a .556 millimeter Galil, which he thought might have come from Israel. The previous week he'd been involved in a two-hour gunfight with some Sandinistas, trading bullets across the river. "The Contras saved you from death," he assured us. "And your man from the CIA."

"The American," the Englishman said. "The one with red hair."

"I never met him," the Captain said, "I don't know his hair."

"But he's the one, I'm sure of it. CIA . . . Well, it was obvious enough I suppose."

"Oh, yeah," I said.

"Still, isn't it shocking. You work," he said to the Captain, "with despicable people."

"Hey," I warned him.

The Captain didn't mind. "It's a business of survival," he said amicably. "If a guy wants to kill you, before you do something bad to me, then—I want to help him kill you. The Contras are good people. Sandinistas are very bad."

"It's that simple, is it."

"Yes, it feels very uncomplicated to me."

"Well . . . Hadn't we better find a hotel?" the Englishman said to me.

"The Señorita will find a hotel herself," the Captain said. "You have to come with us and be arrested."

THE NIGHT was muggy and the wind had stopped. There was an odor from the Río San Juan. This close to the water the mosquitos were bad, and so I kept walking. The middle of the town of Los Chiles was a vacant city block with a patch across it and a few trees interrupting its level lawn. This space was hemmed around by a concrete sidewalk that the citizens were using, in twos and three and fours, to take a little of the night air. Right across the street was the church, a low modern building more like a warehouse than a place of worship. Something must have been scheduled; its doors were thrown wide and it was bright inside. But either the people hadn't come yet or they'd already left the place, because the benches stood empty.

I had a gin and tonic and half a chicken in a dark restaurant. My eyes felt as if they'd been baked and I could hardly hold my head up. I concentrated on these sensations and felt nothing at all to speak of about the Englishman or his trouble.

I spent the night at the Hotel Río Frío, down by the water, in a room the size of a closet. Next door was a station of the Guardia Rural. They hung around up there on the balcony, slapping at bugs and talking, keeping an old recoilless rifle pointed over the railing toward the river. He was probably in there, the Englishman, unless they'd turned him over to the Guardia Civil or the OIJ.

The next morning it rained. I sat in a *soda* eating fried eggs and drinking Coca-Cola. The decor was familiar: on the wall an inexpensive high-gloss print of Jesus Christ surrounded by his pals at the Last Supper, and another print of bulldogs in vests and derby hats, with cigars in their mouths, playing poker on a train. The proprietor was an older man of the Laughing Buddha type. He sat at the rickety table beside mine and played his radio for me. I asked him to leave me alone.

I was still exhausted. I napped, and dreamed I saw the soldiers coming for him, and the redheaded CIA man and another all too obvious American, who was showing the redhead his camera as they walked along together. Such a simple detail, their heads bent toward that object, but its pointlessness gave so much reality to the dream that when my eyes opened and I saw the rows of bottles and various unmatched worm-eaten tablecloths around me I insisted to myself, "That wasn't a dream, somewhere that was really happening, and I saw it."

The rain was falling harder outside and the damp was blowing in—the place had only two walls, the rest was wide-open.

About fifteen minutes after I woke from this strange dream, the redheaded American man came in accompanied by the Costa Rican from the OIJ, both of them wearing dripping ponchos of bright yellow. "You look very much a team," I said to the American.

He only shrugged, reanimating the flow of water from his poncho, and shut his eyes with a certain weariness. But the Costa Rican, who appeared very happy, said, "We are an unbeatable team."

They both shook the water from their ponchos and sat down without taking them off. I saw with some relief that we wouldn't be long about our business.

The American held up two fingers to the proprietor as if hexing him. "Two beers. And give me a napkin."

"English? North American?" the proprietor said.

"He wants a cloth to wipe his face," the Costa Rican said.

"I'll give him a napkin. What else does he want?"

"Two beers," the Costa Rican told him.

"I don't speak English," the fat, smiling proprietor said to the American in Spanish as he set down the glass before him. "Nobody will teach me how to speak it."

"He doesn't speak English," the Costa Rican translated for the American.

"Terrible beer," the American said after he'd tried some. He sat back and waited pleasantly, one leg draped over the other and his hands folded in his yellow lap, a bead of foam clinging to his moustache at the corner of his mouth. He was looking at the Costa Rican.

"I don't like people like you," the Costa Rican told me. "I don't like giving you money." But no amount of irritation was going to dull his sense of triumph. His face shone as he reached under his poncho and then handed me a manila envelope with that unmistakeable heft to it—inside was cash.

His contempt made it easier to take the money.

The American had with him a leather satchel which he put on the table and wiped with the cloth.

He opened it and took out a sheet of paper.

"One more thing for you to sign."

Unbelievable. I just looked at him.

"It's a nuisance, isn't it?" he said.

I signed my name to it and asked him for a match, drawing out a cigaret, and he gave me a light. I handed him the paper.

When I thought of asking him, now that it was all done and ended, what would happen to the Englishman, I had no more strength to do it than if my blood had turned to water. "I'm depressed," I told him. It was stupid, reaching out to him for comfort. He closed up his satchel.

The OIJ man had paid for the beers and stood up.

"Vaya con Dios," I said bitterly.

He nodded to me and pulled up his yellow hood. I looked away.

The American was staring at me with moisture all over his forehead, it was unbearable. I thought he had something to say to me, I was sure he had some piece of news about the Englishman. But then I realized he only wanted to go on watching me suffer. "Maybe they'll give you a commendation in Washington," I said; I wanted to offer the thought of some future satisfaction in exchange for whatever he was taking from me now. The sound of words shook loose his gaze. He followed the Costa Rican out into the rain.

M A Y B E I fell asleep in the restaurant, but in any case I dreamed this goodbye: almost verbatim it was the conversation we'd actually had when the Guardia Captain had arrested him the night before:

I was sneaking off—but the Englishman caught me: "Where are you going . . ."

"I thought I'd grab a bus south."

"You mean we're over. You've done something to free yourself. You're free."

I chattered back at him, but I couldn't hear anything I said.

He said: "And I'm caught, I'm caught, I'm still here."

I was in that town just a day. In the afternoon I got ready to take the bus out of Los Chiles—it was waiting right out in the muddy street before the Guardia station, next door to the hotel—nicer than Nicaraguan buses; nevertheless quite similar to a wooden crate. My hair was still wet from the shower.

But the most terrible thing happened. When I came out of my little cubicle of a room at the Río Frío Hotel, he was there, coming down the corridor.

A pair of Guardia were with him, but not the ones from last night.

I was so confused I actually turned around and tried, for a brief and most ridiculous couple of seconds, to pretend I hadn't seen him or hadn't recognized him or something like that.

"What are you doing here?" I asked him.

"They're letting me use the telephone. It's the only one in the entire town, or so I gather."

If you'd taken me out in the town square and stripped me, set me on fire . . . No punishment could have been more fitting or awful than to be trapped here with him in this narrow corridor.

I started backing up toward the bathrooms and desk and phone, because we were going to have to *touch* brushing past one another if we simply kept going.

"What are you planning to do now?" he said.

"Oh, God—I don't know," I said, "settle down in some nice community someplace and watch the little boys grow up . . ."

"I'm the one who changes, who experiences insight," he said now.

Oh, Jesus.

"There'll never be an England," I told him.

Think of the monster he must have been on Earth, imagine the concentration camps, the oven doors he must have slammed, the screams he must have turned his back on, dusting off his hands, to be sentenced to follow around a quick-change artist like me with his heart cracked and the saliva rolling down off his tongue—that, that right there, that's the kind of person who always gets humiliated . . .

"What do you want me to *do?*"

"You might let us pass," he said.

I WENT to the seaside resort—call it a village—of Playas del Coco, and I wouldn't go on to mention it, except that the Englishman kept figuring so boldly in my life. Nightly he wandered through the shambles of my dreams, dripping with chains, rarely getting a central role but always around, and three or four times I woke to find myself standing upright in the middle of my room at the Playas Hotel, as wet and salty as the ocean seething quietly in its own bed just yards away. I'd sworn off drinking, not for the first or last time—that was the cause of these lurid dreams and night-sweats; in the middle of one such episode, when I turned on the light before washing it all off me in the shower, I found a blue crab the size of a plate crawling up from the drain . . . I ran from the room, collapsed naked on the walk outside, and screamed and screamed until the lights came on in the neighboring bungalows and the desk lady's husband came and carried the thing away to have it cooked. I felt that the Englishman was calling out to me from the edges of these dreams, "I'm dying to meet you . . ." I'm dying to meet you . . . What an awful thing to say. But this hallucination seemed to get in the way of my waking hours, and I started looking for him everywhere. Half of me remembered he was only a dream now; but half of me believed he'd come to town . . .

I dreamed they were boiling him alive. I watched his face

develop like a photograph in a swirl of chemicals. In the hospital I heard his wife screaming yes, that's his face, that's finally his face . . .

Playas del Coco is a restful spot, having that purposeless tropical ambience, that sugary irrelevance in which every night is one night. Mainly it's a stretch of beach between two humps of hill, a cove, I guess. I lay out in the sun to be healed by the motion of coconuts rolled up and back by waves, crabs scuttling around and digging into the dark beach, schools of tiny fish pecking my ankles. The beach was greyish, composed of a volcanic silt that puffed up in a powdery mist around my ankles when I went wading. Not entirely appealing—but oh! the soldiers weren't going to come down from the mountains and bayonet you. And with these people, the color of my passport wasn't interchangeable with the smell of blood. I stayed out until the sun came over the eastward rock about the same time every morning and pierced every grain of sand and leaf. Then it was a little too hot for the beach.

The village has a couple of nice restaurants and also its slummier section, with foot-high homemade bridges wobbling above rivulets of sewage, where the bar stays open even in the rainy season. One of those places where the alcoholic expatriates and Costa Ricans pal around together woozily and argue over the antique jukebox—anyway it boasted an all-Latin selection of 45's.

Only these losers were around. Real people came here in the winter, the dry season—not in August.

The day after I fell off the wagon again—was it a week or so I'd been there by then?—I wandered the town convinced I'd seen the Englishman somewhere the night before—where could it have been? Being hung over made me feel as if I were dreaming . . . I heard him calling from the periphery of things, *I'm dying to meet you . . .*

It was pouring rain—when I get to San José, I promised myself, it won't rain like this.

The town was about five blocks long and one block wide. Inside of ten minutes I'd been everywhere. Places weren't open, there was nothing to see, I was sopping wet and shivering with a chill. I followed a sign to a chapel off the beaten track—in the bush, in fact, down a muddy, depressing, and increasingly unnavigable dirt path. I took off my shoes and went barefoot, the shoes were useless against such deep muck. I needed to get out of the rain, I realized—where was this chapel?—soon enough I'd be in the arms of the Lord, so to speak, out of the unbelievable wet . . . But it wasn't a cozy little chapel at all, it was open to the air, six rows of benches facing a big, rude cross under a thatched roof, and the wilted wreaths and incomprehensible badges, fronds, ribbons, and emblems all over the altar, the insane bric-a-brac of Centroamerican jungle homage—dressed in such paraphernalia it looked the scene of a combined virgin sacrifice and Boy Scout meeting—chilly and damp, and the beaded strings of rain coming down loud as a waterfall on all four sides. And there I had a revelation.

Nothing fancy, but now I knew: It's not enough to observe. It's never enough to observe suffering. With my eyes open I have to let that suffering pay for me. I have to confess, alone in these solitary places, unheard in the roaring rain, that the suffering of the afflicted pays for me. Either I'm Christ or I'm Judas: it's kill or be killed . . .

Are you the Christ? One of us has to be . . .

In a sense I was playacting, but in another sense I was trying to communicate something to myself . . . My mind turned over random events of the night before. There'd been a dogfight in the dirty café at the end of the street, and then a party because one of the barmaids was quitting to get married. And I had a stupid idea that in the course of it someone had delivered a message to me from the Englishman, I couldn't quite remember what it was. I couldn't quite remember the messenger.

I went back to Playas proper and started looking for him, half histrionically, half seriously—but the *soda* was closed, its awning fallen over its face, and the café of last night's wedding party was shut for the rest of the stormy afternoon, and the street outside it was empty . . . It was just a pouring-down rain with nobody in it, and the water running down the road in veins and jostling the fallen coconuts in front of the café.

Well, I'd been *so* terrified of crossing the border, but there was nothing on the other side, just me . . .

s o ; n o w ? —it's none of your business, but the winter finds me pursuing culture in San José, the capital of Costa Rica. I spend my afternoons in the café at the Teatro Nacional, where the waiters do everything to please you but suck your toes; and they don't turn up with the check in their hands the second your café con leche is gone, either. I couldn't bring myself to go back to New York now, even if I could raise the fare. Besides, where I live I can speak all the Manhattan bastard Spanglish I want to with my building's owner . . . I'm staying in reasonable comfort at the United States Hotel. It isn't by any means the Amstel, which is the nicest one downtown, but it's kind of homey, the proprietor isn't at all Centroamericano mellow, he's from Panama by way of the Lower East Side and has the idea no non-paying humans should appear anywhere near where he's leading his life. Don't ask me why he thinks any of his neighbors can read English; but he's put up a little sign over the entrance that says DO NOT STANDING IN FRONT OR JANG AROUND IN DOORSTEP, the same as he did, we can depend on it, above the door of his tenement down on Avenue B.

I spend long evenings at the Key Largo, the infamous supper club where you can't get supper . . . It's set back from the street, only a few doors down from the Hotel Amstel, in its own small misty jungle, with the loneliest green neon sign on

Earth clutching the corner of the building. The grounds are dark and dangerous, but inside there's too much light—they have to keep an eye on the customers. I stand aside, with the other girls, and I drink when invited; upstairs there are rooms; sometimes I leave with a man, sometimes I come back, often I go home . . . And there's never any trouble, nobody insists on representing me, nobody abuses me; I've never been spoken to unkindly.

I'm a favorite of the less widely travelled Americans, the young men who would never pay for love in Kansas, and I'm hated and desired by those more sinister—the man I begin with this evening, for example, a knobby-jointed Alabaman off an Air Force or Navy base in Panama or Puerto Rico with a trembling puppy-dog earnestness I've learned not to mistake for innocence . . . So much character expressed in a face made of absolutely nothing!—no eyes, no nose, no mouth . . . I rib him that if things fall the wrong direction, he'll have to come back here some fine day in an official capacity and level all the buildings and destroy all these people he's been dancing with. "God, I am sure as shit ready for a lady who speaks English," he says, burning like a human flame, "but do you have to blame me about mischief I haven't gotten into yet?" We dance and kiss. His shirt smells brand-new and tainted with the perspiration of his celibacy. He holds me at arm's length a minute, reading my face, and then he puts everything to rest with a certain smoothing gesture of the hands: "I do a job. I don't know anything but my job."

"Same here."

He stands back and watches me dance . . . I stay away from the guitarist so as to avoid his simpering degenerate requests for money. Does he really think we all came in here to hand the colones away? If I had the price of dinner to begin with I wouldn't be in here shaking my money-maker for these looped Caribbean refugees.

He takes me to the bar, and we lean against it. The señoritas in their lively dresses line the walls, somewhat like umbrellas at a funeral . . .

"You got a name?"

"What on earth would I do with something like that?"

The tall black bartender, wearing a white shirt of arctic crispness, delivers me a drink with those gentle hands of his.

"It's the beautiful New York señorita," he says—he's supposedly from Limón, but he's got no accent. "Did you know you got out of here last night with a tab still hanging, bunny?"

Behind him is a window fixed with black wrought iron. The building floats in a cypress swamp, a mossy branch and waxy ivy visible in the green effulgence of the little neon sign outside . . .

"A hundred and fifty?" he says. "Gin tonic and two beers? Does it register?"

"Oh." Last night I'd been angry at him, can't remember why, but justice had cried out that I stiff his suave black ass . . .

"A hundred and fifty. Are you on it?"

"Right, sure, sorry, honey, sorry." I pay him out of my purse.

"Hey, it's not a dilemma." Now that he has his money, it's not a dilemma. "Are you fixed all right? Do you need a little help this week?"

"She's with me, dude," the G.I. says.

"Then I'm happy. She's in very good hands."

The G.I. ignores him, wooing me. "Do you know what's the biggest cause of divorce? Marriage," he fucking opines.

After a while he loses interest in me and drifts away . . .

And then I see another one come in. I've been waiting for him. You know who.

Here he is.

And I say here he is, he's on a roll, he's wired for a win, he's tuned to every known vibration.

Oh, those familiar eyeglasses giving him the faceless face of Clark Kent! . . . But take them off and he is by no means Superman. The way he holds himself there's no mistaking him. Does he have a bit of a tan?

Isn't it him? Or maybe it is. It is. It isn't. But it's him . . .

No, I'm wrong. The accent is all wrong. But he does converse in English. Unbelievable striking fucking similarity, knock you right out, it's the glasses . . .

Those are actually *the* glasses, not a similar pair, but actually the Englishman's glasses on this stranger's face.

He's stolen them off the corpse or out of a prison laundry or bought them from a torturer . . .

"Por favor? Sí?" He lets me look through them—but they aren't the same glasses at all. It isn't at all the kind of view you get through the *real* glasses, these don't make things more distant and crisp but fat, grotesque and not exactly substantial . . . Through these eyes every object is a cloud.

Just to tease him, I pretend I can't speak English. He's forced to make ridiculous signatures in the air with his hands. He has to be a regular monkey, getting his dirty ideas across.

He offers to take me to dinner, but he's a cheap bastard . . .

In no time he and I are eating tacos chinos, that's what they call egg rolls down here, with my friend Esmeralda in a Chinese restaurant and talking to a beggar-boy who's just handed us a well-written letter from his mom. "*Estimados Señores,*" this letter begins, and goes on to say she's raising a large number of children, well whose fault is that, and delivers a little lecture on the subject of her income versus her obligations. Honey, don't you know you've got one of the world's most negotiable instruments right there between your legs?

If you'd made them pay you wouldn't be home arthritically copying out these tearful communications for your bastard children to read to people a great deal more fortunate and quite a bit smarter than you . . . Just the same, we slip him a twenty and I figure, Let the miniaturized sociopath eat my egg roll, even in my line of work I've never been so desperate as to take anything quite like *this* in my mouth. None of the Chinks in this establishment has ever been to China, I'm prepared to insist this is true.

Before this little monkey eats, he counts his money and turns in his change for bills. The egg rolls just sit there in front of him, getting cold. Now we see he's got a wad of cash in those little shorts of his bigger than my purse would hold—this kid has thousands. Don't ask me how he fits it in his pockets, it's a miracle his pants don't plummet to his ankles when he walks. "Ho, Malo," I say, "bueno!"

But I'm being too familiar. "Don't call me Malo," he says.

"Is this crippled duck still here?" I ask Esmeralda, putting my hand on the customer's thigh.

The customer wants to do it with two women. He doesn't have much money. He's a cheap bastard.

It's uncanny how this mind-blown welder—for that's what he is, a welder from Miami with an overseas contract, gone nuts—brings to mind the Englishman, and I wonder what became of my friend from London, and how bad it hurt . . . But you know who this lint-collector really reminds me of? Humphrey Bogart. There's something sideways and not altogether repellent about his glance, and something Bogart-like in the pain of his wince.

A clear reminiscence of Humphrey Bogart seems to inform the modes and styles and even the gestures tonight . . . Whatsisname, the long black bartender without a trace of an accent, shaking drinks . . .

And Esmeralda, the red-dressed high-class prostitute—she might have stepped out from behind a potted palm in a Hollywood lounge, 1953 . . . Who knows where they get it; after all, the movie houses are showing, Spanish-dubbed, whatever's current Stateside. Maybe they watch a lot of Humphrey Bogart on TV.

Maybe the air of this place just seizes and holds as long as it can that pre-Castro Havanan tang, or possibly it drifted down here years ago and got lost not unlike so many of us, hey . . .

He's been spilling his pay out behind him for days, all he's got is about 1,800—I'd want two grand for me alone. He keeps saying, "Let's do it three ways, c'mon, tres—tu, yo, una otra, Señorita comprende, sí?"

Esmeralda, or whatever her name is, isn't interested.

He wants me to find another, offering me 1,500 colones. I cost a lot more than that, I'm a rarity, without a drop of Indian blood . . . I'm white as dice . . .

We go down to one of the sleazier spots, next door to a massage parlor, looking for a second girl. In the dark he looks just like the Englishman. I start weeping, I'm the sentimental sort . . . So we dicker, and like every North American, he's heartbroken to talk of money and love together.

The only one I can foozle into it cheaply enough to make it worth my while is Mona Lisa, who has a little difficulty with opiates and also alcohol, anything, for that matter, that will chemically alter her outlook and produce fog inside her head . . .

I always think of her as Mona Lisa because she has a secretive, beautiful smile that says, "It's over—why are we still here?" She keeps scratching her nose and falling asleep.

Next door they have rooms. The three of us go out together. In the kitchen a chubby fellow cleans a pistol while he talks to the radio. No . . . There's a woman sitting against the wall by the radio.

"Hello, people," the North American tells them.

He has to pay three hundred for the bed.

He doesn't mind, he's got plenty, he's been holding out on us. And he pays the two of us, like an absolute dildo, in advance. We all undress. Good old Mona Lisa, scratching her nose, falls back beside me on the bed. "Tonight I'm lopsided," she tells me.

And the naked welder kneels above us. Maybe he'll kill us. Maybe this is the maniac we've all been waiting for.

In this near-dark he's quite handsome. "Muy lindo," I say to Mona Lisa, and she agrees . . . But he's a miserable sissy, as limp and useless between his legs as a long wet hair. The night is cool, yet the sweat breaks out on him. Mona Lisa doesn't go in for a lot of English, and I keep on pretending I don't speak it, either . . . He's reduced to a savage state, naked, signalling with his hands. By all kinds of ridiculous gestures and in great embarrassment he tries to get one of us to fellate him. We don't know what he's talking about. Hon, you shouldn't have paid up front . . . He tries to ignore his failure, he tries to fake it, he tries to laugh it off, he tries to explain himself. He's getting humiliated just like the other one, I can smell him boiling in a swirl of the same emotions that vaporized the Britisher . . .

"I think I'll stay here tonight," Mona Lisa says to me. "I'm feeling sleepy."

"He paid enough. They'll let you stay."

"He paid three hundred," she recalls fondly.

And will you just *observe* how this character is being tortured? He looks more and more like the Englishman. He doesn't see the dark world's innumerable eyes observing. Two young women submitted before his wishes—and he's useless above them, on his knees on the bed, useless!

The speechless poet, the blind painter—a tingling in the sculptor's amputated hands . . .

Holy Jesus, what this guy must have done in his time on Earth . . . To be put here with his dreams, but not himself, made substance . . .

A NOTE ON THE TYPE

The text of this book was set in Electra, a typeface designed by
W(illiam) A(ddison) Dwiggins for the Mergenthaler Linotype
company and first made available in 1935. Electra cannot be
classified as either "modern" or "old-style." It is not based on
any historical model, and hence does not echo any particular
period or style of type design. It avoids the extreme contrast
between thick and thin elements that marks most modern faces,
and is without eccentricities that interfere with reading. In
general, Electra is a simple, readable typeface that attempts to
give a feeling of fluidity, power, and speed.

Composed by Maryland Linotype Composition Company,
Baltimore, Maryland

Printed and bound by R. R. Donnelley & Sons,
Harrisonburg, Virginia

Typography and binding design by
Dorothy Schmiderer